T...

BLACK-...

by Cindy Gerard

Millionaire Jacob Thorne has gotten on Christine Travers's last nerve! She has no time for his teasing flirtation. But when they butt heads at an auction, Jake embarks on a seduction that will prove she has needs—womanly needs— that only *he* can satisfy.

SILHOUETTE DESIRE IS PROUD TO PRESENT

TEXAS Cattleman's Club

The Secret Diary

A new drama unfolds for six of the state's wealthiest bachelors.

* * *

And don't miss

LESS-THAN-INNOCENT-INVITATION

by Shirley Rogers

The second installment of the Texas Cattleman's Club: The Secret Diary series.

Available next month in Silhouette Desire!

Dear Reader,

July is a month known for its heat and fireworks, as well as the perfect time to take that vacation. Well, why not take a break and enjoy some hot sparks with a Silhouette Desire? We've got six extraordinary romances to share with you this month, starting with *Betrayed Birthright* by Sheri WhiteFeather. This seventh title in our outstanding DYNASTIES: THE ASHTONS series is sure to reveal some unbelievable facts about this scandalous family.

USA TODAY bestselling author Maureen Child wraps up her fabulous THREE-WAY WAGER series with *The Last Reilly Standing.* Or is he getting down on bended knee? And while some series are coming to a close, new ones are just beginning, such as our latest installment of the TEXAS CATTLEMAN'S CLUB: THE SECRET DIARY. Cindy Gerard kicks off this six-book continuity with *Black-Tie Seduction.* Also starting this month is Bronwyn Jameson's PRINCES OF THE OUTBACK. These Australian hunks really need to be tamed, beginning with *The Rugged Loner.*

A desert beauty in love with a tempting beast. That's the theme of Nalini Singh's newest release, *Craving Beauty*—a story not to be missed. And the need to break a long-standing family curse leads to an attraction that's just *Like Lightning,* an outstanding romance by Charlene Sands.

Here's hoping you enjoy all the fireworks Silhouette Desire has to offer you…this month and all year long!

Best,

Melissa Jeglinski

Melissa Jeglinski
Senior Editor
Silhouette Desire

Please address questions and book requests to:
Silhouette Reader Service
U.S.: 3010 Walden Ave., P.O. Box 1325, Buffalo, NY 14269
Canadian: P.O. Box 609, Fort Erie, Ont. L2A 5X3

Black-Tie Seduction

CINDY GERARD

Silhouette® Desire

Published by Silhouette Books

America's Publisher of Contemporary Romance

Special thanks and acknowledgment are given
to Cindy Gerard for her contribution to the
TEXAS CATTLEMAN'S CLUB:
THE SECRET DIARY series.

 SILHOUETTE BOOKS

ISBN 0-373-76665-3

BLACK-TIE SEDUCTION

Visit Silhouette Books at www.eHarlequin.com

Printed in U.S.A.

Books by Cindy Gerard

Silhouette Desire

The Cowboy Takes a Lady #957
Lucas: The Loner #975
*The Bride Wore Blue #1012
*A Bride for Abel Greene #1052
*A Bride for Crimson Falls #1076
†The Outlaw's Wife #1175
†Marriage, Outlaw Style #1185
†The Outlaw Jesse James #1198
Lone Star Prince #1256
In His Loving Arms #1293
Lone Star Knight #1353

The Bridal Arrangement #1392
The Secret Baby Bond #1460
Taming the Outlaw #1465
The Librarian's Passionate
   Knight #1525
Tempting the Tycoon #1539
Breathless for the Bachelor #1564
Storm of Seduction #1583
Between Midnight and
   Morning #1630
Black-Tie Seduction #1665

*Northern Lights Brides
†Outlaw Hearts

Silhouette Books

Family Secrets
The Bluewater Affair

CINDY GERARD

Since her first release in 1991 hit the National #1 slot on the Waldenbooks bestseller list, Cindy Gerard has repeatedly made appearances on several bestseller lists, including *USA TODAY*.

With numerous industry awards to her credit—among them the Romance Writers of America's RITA® Award and the National Reader's Choice Award—this former Golden Heart finalist and repeat *Romantic Times* nominee is the real deal. As one book reviewer put it, "Cindy Gerard provides everything romance readers want in a love story—passion, gut-wrenching emotion, intriguing characters and a captivating plot. This storyteller extraordinaire delivers all of this and more!"

Cindy and her husband, Tom, live in the Midwest on a minifarm with quarter horses, cats and two very spoiled dogs. When she's not writing, she enjoys reading, traveling and spending time at their cabin in northern Minnesota unwinding with family and friends. Cindy loves to hear from her readers and invites you to visit her Web site at www.cindygerard.com.

This book is dedicated to the fabulous women
who worked so hard to make this new segment
of the Texas Cattleman's Club saga the best yet!
Shirley Rogers, Brenda Jackson, Michelle Celmer,
Sara Orwig and Kristi Gold.
Ladies, it's been my great pleasure!

Prologue

From the diary of Jessamine Golden
July 4, 1905

Dear Diary,
Today my life changed. It came out of the blue. Like a lightning strike in the midst of a sunset storm or the fireworks lighting up the sky during tonight's celebration of our country's independence. I'm not sure how else to describe what happened to me when I first set eyes on Brad Webster—or how to describe the clash of wills when he drew me aside and told me how things were going to be.

"I run a clean town," he said. "I don't want any trouble from you."

He looked stern and angry and so very serious when he talked to me. And yet he didn't arrest me, this man who walks on the opposite path that fate has set for me.

Sheriff Brad Webster. Just writing his name makes my heart kick around inside my chest like a string of wild ponies. Saying it out loud makes my fingers tremble and my face flush hot and sends strange warm flames licking through my belly. You'd think I'd been smoking locoweed. And it is *loco* for me to be so obsessed by him.

But despite his anger at me, he is the most beautiful man…if a man can be called beautiful. I remember some years ago Daddy and I were riding strays and we came upon this herd of wild mustangs. The stallion was big and ink-black and, oh, he was the prettiest thing I'd ever seen. Sleek and muscled, tall and strong. One look in that big guy's eyes and you knew he was proud and brave.

That's what I thought when I saw the sheriff. Like that wild stallion, he is proud and brave. His hair is ink-black. His eyes are the most fascinating Texas-sky-blue. And tall. Lordy, is that man tall. But he's no beanpole. Oh, no. He's got the build of a working man. And he's a man who believes in duty.

Duty. His duty is why I must stop carrying on

about him so. Brad Webster wears a badge that says he's the law. And everything about the way he carries himself says he is as loyal to the law as I am loyal to the cause that has taken me on the wrong side of it.

Dear, dear diary. Is there anything in life that is fair? Why does everything have to be so hard? I have met a man who makes me want to forget what drove me to a life of crime. But I can't forget. I can't. Just as I can't forget that this amazing, beautiful man may be forced, by duty, to end my very life. Even worse, I may be forced to end his.

One

One man's trash. Another man's treasure.

The old cliché wound around inside Christine Travers's head like a coil of barbwire as she stared, disbelieving, at the treasure she'd just discovered.

The good folks of Royal, Texas, had dug deep into their basements and attics to come up with items to donate to tonight's auction. There were antique crystal pieces. Complete china sets. Magazines that dated back to the early nineteenth century. Furniture and painstakingly hand-stitched quilts. And then there was this box.

Her breath stalled. Her heart beat so fast and so hard, she was afraid she might pass out. Right here. Right smack in the middle of this crowd of upper-crust residents, including a large contingent of Texas Cattleman's Club members—the infamous and elite philanthropic organization that had staged tonight's fund-raising auction to benefit Royal's upcoming one hundred and twenty-fifth anniversary celebration.

So, no. Passing out would not be good form any way you sliced it. And the last thing she would ever want to do was bring attention to herself—for any reason.

Okay, Christine. Settle down. Take a deep breath. Another.

Steadier now, with her fingers only marginally tingling, she glanced around the auction house to see if anyone was watching her with an odd expression—a sure sign she'd either screamed out loud, jumped up and down or done something equally ridiculous and brought unwanted attention to herself. And to her amazing find.

A relieved sigh eddied out when no one seemed to notice her excitement. Almost everyone who had turned out was busy browsing. Well, almost everyone.

Some of the Cattleman's Club members, including Jacob Thorne, she'd noticed with dismay, were laughing and joking by the bar across the room.

Why did he have to be here?

Christine made it a point to avoid Jacob Thorne. If he spotted her tonight, she had no doubt that, true to form, he'd make it his personal mission to give her ten different kinds of grief. What she'd ever done to deserve his teasing and goading—other than help save his miserable life—was beyond her.

Well, she wasn't going to think about him tonight. She had another meatier, much more exciting matter to attend to. Rows and rows of tables were filled with items that would soon be up for bid. Among those items Christine had found buried treasure—or the next best thing to it. The contents of this box, according to the notation, came from the late Jonathan Devlin's attic.

Oh. My. God.

"Is it hot in here?" Christine asked her friend, Alison Lind, as she fussed with her plain white blouse that she'd buttoned all the way up to her neck.

"It's Texas. It's July," Alison said, deadpan. Her dark eyes sparkled in her pretty chocolate-brown face. While Christine was usually cautious about opening herself up to someone, she'd sensed a kindred spirit in Alison. They'd met at a self-defense class a few months ago and had been fast friends since.

"Okay. Rhetorical question," Christine conceded. "It just seemed extra warm there for a minute."

Alison gave her friend a look and an "Uh-huh," then walked on ahead of Christine toward a bolt of red satin.

"All right," Christine whispered to herself and wiped damp palms on her tailored navy slacks. "Get a grip."

Act cool. Don't let on that you may have just discovered what must have appeared to be nothing more than an old, musty-smelling saddlebag to the late Jonathan Devlin's family. Nothing more than a novelty item someone might want to bid on to decorate a bar or a tack room—instead of a major historical find.

Well, they could bid, she thought fiercely, but she was going to leave here with the contents of this box. That's because she knew something no one else did. She was ninety-nine-point-nine percent certain that she knew who the saddlebag had once belonged to.

"What's got you so fidgety?" Alison asked, wandering back to Christine's side. She tried to peek into the box.

Christine quickly flipped the lid shut.

"Can you keep a secret?" Christine whispered, cutting a covert glance around her.

Alison frowned. "If the secret is that you're having a minor manic episode, no, I don't think so. The paramedics who treat you will need details."

Ignoring her friend's sarcasm, Christine gripped Alison's arm and pulled her close. She lifted the lid on the box. The smell of old leather and dust seeped into the air. "See this saddlebag?"

"Oh—I get to look inside now?"

Christine pulled a face. "Yes, you get to look inside."

Still acting wary, Alison did.

"Notice the rose tooled on the cover flap?"

From Alison she got a slow, skeptical nod.

"The rose is what drew my attention. So I checked inside the bag," Christine confided in a low voice, "and found a pair of six-shooters. *Old* six-shooters, with roses carved into the ivory handles."

"And..." Alison said in a leading tone as Christine cast more worried looks around them.

"And there's also a delicate little purse. Again—old.

Rose-colored—with what appear to be rose petals inside. Plus—" she huddled up with Alison and whispered "—there's a map."

She snatched Alison's hand back with an apologetic look when Alison started to reach inside the saddlebag. "A map with hearts and roses twining around the edge."

"Okay. I'll play along," Alison said, still frowning as though she thought Christine had blown a circuit. "I'm guessing there's some major significance to all these roses?"

"You don't know the half of it," Christine said. "I'm positive these things once belonged to Jessamine Golden."

When Alison made a "who?" face, Christine closed the box, then tugged Alison away from the table and hustled her into the line of people waiting to acquire bidding numbers.

"Jessamine Golden is a legend in Royal," she explained in a low voice so no one would overhear. "She was an outlaw a hundred years ago who not only stole the heart of the town sheriff, Brad Webster, but legend has it that she also stole a huge gold shipment and hid the treasure somewhere in the Royal area. And she *loved* roses.

"Thanks," she said absently when the clerk gave her a paddle with a number on it. She walked Alison to the row of seats lined up in front of the podium where the bidding was already under way.

"Anyway, the rest of the story is that the mayor of Royal back then was Edgar Halifax—"

"Halifax?" Alison interrupted. "Any relation to Gretchen Halifax, our illustrious city councilwoman?"

Gretchen Halifax wasn't an *illustrious* anything except in her own mind, and both women knew it, but Christine didn't want to get sidetracked with talk about Gretchen. She'd had to deal with Gretchen on the new Edgar Halifax display at the museum and that had been more than enough exposure to the woman. Christine always was willing to give people the benefit of the doubt, but in this case the stories about Gretchen appeared to be true. The councilwoman was pompous and self-important and on more than one occasion had been very condescending toward Christine.

"Yes, I think Gretchen is some distant relative, but the point is Edgar Halifax and his men were supposedly killed by Jessamine Golden over the stolen gold. There's also speculation that Jessamine killed the sheriff, too, because when she disappeared, neither one of them was ever heard from again. And the gold was never found."

Christine tugged Alison down on the chair beside her, facing the auctioneer. "I think the map in those saddlebags is a map to where Jess hid the gold!" she whispered fiercely.

Alison searched her friend's face. "All right. Did you eat an entire bag of chocolate before you came here?"

The look on Alison's face coupled with her silly question finally made Christine laugh. "No," she assured her friend; "I did *not* eat any chocolate, and will you quit looking at me like I'm an alien? I'm serious.

You know that I volunteer time at the Royal Historical Society when I'm not pulling double shifts at the hospital. I do a lot of research there, and Jess Golden's story caught my attention. And, Alison, I swear those have to be Jess's things in that box that came out of Jonathan Devlin's attic."

"Out of Jonathan Devlin's attic?" Alison shook her head. "Boy, the Devlins didn't waste any time clearing out old Jonathan's house. He only died a few days ago—they haven't even buried him yet, have they?"

"Not yet, no. But you know his sister Opal? A month ago, when Jonathan went into a coma, it was expected that he'd never recover. I guess from the start there was no brain activity. Anyway, Opal had been going through his house for weeks in anticipation of his death, setting aside things to put up for auction."

"Gives me warm fuzzies all over thinking about her sorrow over the loss of her brother."

Christine smiled. "Tell me about it. Opal's a sentimental and sympathetic soul all right," she said, matching Alison's sarcasm. "But back to the topic at hand. One of the reasons I'm so convinced these are Jess Golden's things is that for a very brief time—around 1910 or so—she lived in Jonathan Devlin's house."

"Okay," Alison said carefully but looking as if she was a little more on board, "let's say you're right. Let's say those are Jess Golden's things because she left them in the house when she skedaddled out of town after she did her dastardly deed. What then?"

"Then I'm going to buy them," Christine stated emphatically. "For the Historical Society to put on display in the museum. That box contains priceless historical artifacts—not to mention, it might lead to the gold. What a find it would be for the town."

"Well, you'd better get your paddle ready, Miss Supersleuth. They just brought the box to the podium. It's the next item up for bid."

Jake Thorne wasn't sure what it was about Chrissie Travers that lit his fire, but every time he showed up someplace and she was there, it was as though some kinetic energy source set all his senses on supercharge and he homed in on her like a bear scenting honey.

He propped an elbow on the bar where he stood at the side of the room and got comfortable. Then he just enjoyed the hell out of watching her in typical Prissy Chrissie mode, all stiff and proper and tense, while his mind—already shifting into autopilot—started hatching plots to irritate her. Just a little. Because, man, she was some fun when she was riled.

And he ought to know. He'd spent a month in the Royal hospital five years ago after an oil-well fire had knocked him on his ass. The burns hadn't been the worst of his injuries. The smoke and fire inhalation and the resulting damage to his lungs had been. Chrissie had been his respiratory therapist, and once he'd felt human again, he'd found a hundred hot buttons to push on the uptight, serious and tolerate-no-nonsense Chrissie Travers. He was pleased to say that he'd personally pushed at least ninety-nine of them at some time or another.

Her bidding paddle shot up in the air. *Whoa. What have we here?* he wondered when she lifted it above her head. Straight up. No hesitation. As high as she could raise her arm.

Seemed the lady aimed to buy something. Judging by her body language, she meant to have it at any cost.

He watched both Chrissie and the bidding with interest. She cast a flurry of darting looks around her, those big hazel eyes warning off anyone who even looked as if they wanted to raise their paddle. Interesting. The bidding was slow and it looked as though she was going to get the box of, hell, box of rocks for all he knew, for a song.

Or is she? he asked himself and felt the beginnings of an ornery grin. Just as the auctioneer was about to start a "Going, going, gone," with Chrissie as the high bidder, Jake's paddle seemed to sort of pop up in the air, all of its own accord.

Hmm. Looked as though he was in the bidding now, too.

Chrissie's head whipped around, her fine blond hair flying around her face, her big hazel eyes snapping with smoke and hellfire as she searched the room for the culprit who dared to enter the bidding at this late hour.

When her gaze finally landed on him and he acknowledged with a grin and a friendly wave of his paddle that, yeah, he was the one who'd jumped in and spoiled her party, he swore to God lightning zapped out of her ears and shot twin puffs of smoke in its wake.

And when after a fierce flurry of bidding action between them ended with a gavel rap and a resounding, "Sold!" and Jake was the lucky owner of a cardboard box containing he had no idea what, the look she sent him could have set a forest ablaze.

He touched his fingertips to the brim of his tan Resistol, smiled sweetly and swore he heard a word come out of her mouth that he figured prissy Miss Chrissie had never even heard before, let alone used.

Oh, boy. We're gonna have some fun now.

Christine glared at the man sauntering toward her. Jacob Thorne was wearing what he probably thought was an aren't-I-just-as-sexy-as-sin rogue grin that tugged up one corner of his full, mobile lips and dented his incredible dimples. He thought he was something— looking at her as if he was God's greatest gift. As if her heart ought to go pit-a-pat and she ought to get hot all over basking in the glow of his company, as half the women in town did every time he sliced one of his poster-boy smiles their way.

Well, she was hot all right. Bonfire hot. And her heart was pounding. Not some loopy, goofy stutter step but a jackhammer, piston-pumping, so-mad-she-could-hear-each-staccato-beat-in-her-ears-and-feel-it-pulse-all-the-way-to-her-toes pounding. And in that moment she understood why it sometimes became part of the human condition to react to anger with physical violence.

Not that she'd ever stoop that low. She'd experienced enough physical violence in her life. But it didn't hurt to think about exactly how deep she could bury the tip of her boot into Jacob Thorne-in-her-side's shin. And to imagine his grunt of pain, the swelling and the black-and-blue marks when she did.

"Hey, Chrissie," he said, all sweet and sugary, with that sexy, sandpapery voice of his. "You're looking mighty fine tonight. Got a little color in your cheeks for a change. Did you finally take some time for yourself and get out in the sun a bit?"

She tilted her head to the side and glared at him. And he had the nerve to try to be cute. Again.

"Oh. *Not* sun." He made a big show of acting surprised. "You're miffed at me, right? *That's* what put that pretty pink in your cheeks."

For whatever reason, ever since she'd been his respiratory therapist, he seemed to make it his personal mission to tease her unmercifully. Like a big, overgrown bully. He needed to grow up, that's what he needed to do. In the meantime she'd treat him like the kid he was.

"You are *so* not funny. And you are *so* not charming."

She reached out and grabbed Alison's arm, holding her still when she sensed that her friend was about to slink away and avoid certain fireworks.

"Now, how much do you want for it?" she asked

with a clipped nod toward the box he'd tucked under his arm. The box that contained Jessamine Golden's saddlebag and its treasure trove of goodies. The box that had almost been hers for fifty-five bucks until he'd chimed in with his big money and stolen it from her.

He glanced from her to the box. "What's in here that's got you so excited?"

She blinked. Then, outraged, blinked again. "You didn't even know what you were bidding on?"

"Well, no," he said, lifting a shoulder. "I was just trying to make some extra money for the benefit."

"You know what?" Alison said, squirming uneasily and apparently sensing a major showdown. "I think I'll just be going now."

Christine wrapped her fingers tighter around Alison's upper arm and held her where she was. "So why didn't you bid against Ralph Schindler when he was bidding on an antique typewriter? Or Mel Grazier when he bid on a boom box? They've got buckets of moldy money. Why did you have to bid against me?"

"Well," he said, then paused and absently scratched his jaw. "Maybe I figured if you wanted it, it must be something worth having."

She snorted. "Try again."

"No, really. I've always known you to have excellent taste."

"So…that's supposed to be an explanation?"

"More like a compliment."

"More like a crock. You did it just to tick me off."

"Well—" his dark eyes danced in a tan, handsome face "—there is that."

The sound that came out of her could only be described as a growl.

"I've really got to go," Alison said, making another break for it.

This time Christine let her go. It wasn't fair to Alison to make her a party to what could in all probability turn out to be a homicide.

"How much do you want for it?" she repeated only after she was certain she could talk without screeching.

"You want it bad, don't you, Chrissie?"

Oh, he'd just love to see her rise to *that* bait. She was not going to give him the satisfaction of acknowledging the sexual innuendo he'd managed to thread through his seemingly innocent question punctuated with a wicked smile.

"How much?"

"Tell you what," he said, looking if not smug, at least pleased by whatever idea was brewing in his thick head. "How about we cut us a little deal?"

Cut a deal? She'd trust any deal he made about as far as she could shot-put his beefy carcass after she killed him but before they hauled her off to jail. Justifiable homicide would be the worst possible charge they could level.

"I can just about imagine any deal you'd initiate. You haven't changed a bit, have you?"

"Aw, Chrissie. You don't still hold a grudge after all this time, do you?"

Oh, yeah. She held a grudge all right. He made it easy.

"Tell you what, just to show you I'm not so awful," he said, working hard at sounding wounded, "since you want this stuff that badly, I'll just give it to you."

She eyed him with unconcealed suspicion. All six-plus lean feet of him. She couldn't help but notice the way his long brown hair curled slightly at the edges, giving him a sexy boyish appeal. Couldn't help but try to read the thoughts going on behind those summer-blue eyes that were always laughing, always teasing, always making her wonder what made him tick.

Well. Not *always* because she didn't spend that much time thinking about him. At least, she didn't do it intentionally. He sort of sneaked into her thoughts sometimes when she least expected it and caught her off guard.

Like now. Damn, all those wonder-boy good looks had sidetracked her again. Made her forget—if only for a second there—that she was mad and he was the reason.

"Okay. What's the catch?" Skepticism oozed in each word.

"What makes you think there's a catch?"

"Because I wasn't born yesterday?"

"There ya go. You're just as smart as you are pretty."

"Oh, for Pete's sake, save the sugar for someone with a sweet tooth."

He considered her for a moment as if he were thinking about how badly he wanted to embarrass her. Then he very coolly said, "You can have the box of stuff on one condition. Be my date for the anniversary ball."

It took a moment for Christine to process his words. When she finally realized what he was suggesting, her mouth dropped open. Nothing came out.

If he'd told her the condition was to strip and then run through the streets proclaiming she was madly in love with him, she would have been less surprised than she was right now.

And the chances of her agreeing to either condition were exactly the same.

"Boy, that got you thinking," he said, his lean cheeks dimpling. "So, what do you say? How about it?"

He wasn't serious. He couldn't be. Never in a million years would Jake Thorne—Texas Cattleman's Club member and one of the most sought-after bachelors in Royal—waste his time with her, not at something as big as the anniversary ball. Not when all the eligible socialites and darlings of society were lined up like Miss America candidates waiting for him to select one of them as his date for the biggest social event in recent Royal history. Beautiful, wealthy, socially adept women who ran in his circle and would look good on his arm—unlike her, who would look more like a lump of coal than a diamond.

Even though she didn't want it to, it stung that he'd play with her this way when they both knew good and well that, unless he thought he could find some perverse pleasure humiliating her, he'd never in a million years include her on his list of possible dates.

This was just too cruel. And she'd had enough of his goading for one night.

"How about you take your condition and put it where the sun don't shine?"

Then, hating herself for letting him get to her, she turned on her heel and stomped away while his highly amused "Was it something I said?" trailed her across the room.

Two

"**I** don't get it," Alison said the night after the auction as they waited at the back of the room for their self-defense class to start. "What's the problem with going to the anniversary ball with Jake Thorne? It's not like you already have a date. And good grief, girl, the man is a hottie of the major-flame variety. No pun intended."

But it was a pun regardless since Jacob Thorne's stock-in-trade was fighting oil-well fires. Or at least, it used to be his stock-in-trade to fight them until the accident. Everything had changed for him then. He still ran his own company, but from a desk now instead of on the actual site of the fires.

Christine sat down on the mat and fussed with the

laces of her tennis shoes, shoving thoughts of the trauma he'd gone through from her mind.

"He's a hottie all right. Of the inflammatory variety."

"Well, he sure seems to have incited a riot in you."

"We have a history," Christine finally admitted in a weak moment as she pulled her straight shoulder-length hair into a ponytail and clipped it at her nape.

"*No*. I never would have guessed," Alison said, clearly having guessed exactly that.

Christine grinned at her friend's staged surprise.

"What did he do, dump you?"

"No," she said sobering. "He did *not* dump me. We've never even dated."

"Ah. So *that's* the problem. You want to date him."

"Yeah, right," Christine said maybe a little too emphatically.

This time Alison didn't say a word. She just raised an eyebrow and waited.

Christine expelled a weary sigh and rose to her feet. "Okay. The problem," she sputtered, using Alison's words, "is that he's just making fun of me by inviting me to the dance. He's always making fun of me. He taunts and teases and plays on the fact that I had a little crush on him once—a *looonnnggg* time ago—and he keeps exploiting it. You saw how he was at the auction. He didn't want that box for any reason other than because I wanted it. And he didn't ask me to the ball for any other reason than to mock me."

She tugged down her T-shirt, then forked her fingers

through her ponytail, getting mad all over again just thinking about it. "He just loves to push my buttons. I'm getting tired of it."

"I think it's kind of cute," Alison said, then laughed when Christine threw her a disbelieving look. "Well, I do. Because it's all in fun and what it really means is that he has a thing for you."

Christine grunted. "It means that he's childish and sophomoric. And he doesn't have a *thing* for me. I mean, look at me—I'm as far from his type as a male stripper is from mine. He's just…ornery. The man doesn't have a sincere bone in his body. Everything's a joke with him."

"Everything?"

She thought for a moment. "Okay. For instance—he got hurt badly in an oil-well fire five years ago. Smoke and fire inhalation did some heavy-duty damage to his lungs and he spent over a month in the hospital. I was the unlucky one on duty the night they brought him in and I ended up spending a lot of time with him over the course of his recovery."

When some other class members walked in, Christine lowered her voice because she didn't want them to overhear her. And she really didn't want to relive those days in a play-by-play for Alison.

That didn't stop her from thinking about it, though. Jacob Thorne had been one sick puppy. She'd been so worried for him, while he'd been brave and determined to recover and joked his way through the pain and the fear of his prognosis. She'd admired him for it...then formed that unfortunate crush.

She did *not* admire him for it now. Neither did she have a crush on him. Not anymore.

"Anyway, a couple of weeks into his treatment his twin brother, Connor, came to visit him. His *identical* twin," she added to make sure Alison understood. "Long story short, they pulled a switch on me so Jacob—the evil twin— could sneak out of the hospital and go down to the Cattleman's Club for a beer. The end result was that I actually gave a respiratory therapy session to the wrong man!"

She got angry all over again just thinking about it. "He could have caused himself a serious setback pulling a reckless stunt like that."

Alison looked at her as if she was waiting for the punch line. Finally she said, "That's it? That's why you don't like him? The poor guy had been stuck in a hospital bed, sick as a dog. A cold beer and some male company sounded good to him so he pulled a fast one on you to indulge in a tiny little creature comfort?"

"I don't like him," Christine restated, not liking that she felt defensive again, "because he doesn't get it. He doesn't get it that life is not one big lark. Life is serious. Life is real. It's not a game, and you can't just play your way through it the way he does."

For the first time Alison looked at her with no trace of humor. And it was then that Christine realized tears had pooled in her eyes. Embarrassed, she quickly blinked them back.

"Oh, sweetie." Alison reached out, touched her hand. "What happened to you?"

Instantly on edge, Christine pulled her hand away. She wasn't comfortable with touching, even though Alison's touch held compassion and concern—something entirely different than the hard hands that had touched her in anger when she was a child. "I—I don't know what you mean."

"I mean, what happened to you that made you decide life had to be all about work and duty with no room for fun?" Alison pressed gently.

Fortunately for Christina, Mark Hartman, Alison's boss—who was also the self-defense class's instructor and another Texas Cattleman's Club member like Jacob—entered the room at that very moment.

His appearance and the necessity to get down to business saved Christine from opening up like a faucet and spilling out her sordid history to this woman whose insight and empathy had almost broken through defenses she'd kept shored up her entire life.

Christine was appalled with herself when she realized her eyes still stung with tears. She blinked them back and, giving Alison an apologetic look, moved away from her and onto her spot on the practice mat. Christine wished she could talk to her friend about her past. But she couldn't. Not yet.

For the rest of the class she went through the self-defense positions like an automaton, knowing the moves as well as she knew the secret she'd kept from anyone who had ever gotten too close.

She had good reason to know that life was not fun and games. Life was a father who had beaten her and her mother and a mother who drank to escape the pain. Christine hadn't had any escape—only fear—until she'd turned eighteen and finally had been able to run. She'd run as far away as she could from that horrible existence and the memories that sometimes still woke her, trembling, in the night.

That's what had happened to her, she thought as she showered in the locker room later. That's why she sometimes worked double shifts at the hospital, why she took her job as a respiratory therapist so seriously and why she also volunteered to work for the Historical Society. She never wanted to have to depend on anyone but herself. Her work at the hospital gave her that self-sufficiency. Her volunteer work at the Historical Society gave her a sense of community.

Both also gave her something else—something she hadn't expected and hadn't known she'd needed—respectability. Acceptance. A place to belong.

She protected those hard-earned parts of her life. Held them close—held herself aloof to make sure no one got close enough to discover that inside her, there were still strong echoes of a lost and helpless little girl who had always thought she wasn't good enough for her own father to love her. For her own mother to protect her.

She never wanted to feel that sense of helplessness or hopelessness again. Respectability, security and safety. She'd needed them most as a child but had never received them. As an adult, she'd earned them and she never took them for granted.

Life was work. Life was hard. How many times had her father driven that point home? Often enough that she'd absorbed it along with the blows from the back of his hand.

Yeah, she thought pragmatically. Life was hard. But life was also precious.

And that's why she didn't like Jake Thorne, with his life-is-a-lark attitude and his damn-the-torpedoes grin. He took everything for granted. So much so that it puzzled her how someone like him had gotten invited to join the Cattleman's Club—a club that was about duty and honor and public service. And if some of the rumors were to be believed, it was also a club where the members were covertly active in thwarting any number of horrible situations. In fact, she'd heard specific rumors that the club had been instrumental in breaking up a black-market baby network and once had prevented a bloody overthrow of a small European principality. Jacob Thorne just didn't seem to fit the Cattleman's profile.

Fun and games. That seemed to be as deep as he got. She didn't know how to react around someone who was always smiling and joking. The way he'd joked with her the other night.

"Him and his condition," she sputtered under her breath, remembering how he'd told her she could have the saddlebags if she met his condition.

Nothing had changed there, she admitted, as with a

brief hug she begged off Alison's offer to stop at the Royal Diner for a diet soda that was really a ruse to get her to talk. Christine wasn't ready to confide that part of her life with Alison, although she'd come as close to telling her as she had anyone.

Instead she went home. She still wanted the box with Jess Golden's things for the Historical Society. And because this was serious business, she knew what she'd known from the beginning and simply hadn't wanted to admit.

She'd have to give in to Thorne's condition. Eat some crow and call him. Tell him she'd reconsidered. She'd go to his damn ball—so he could have some fun at her expense.

She undressed, brushed and flossed, then slipped into a white cotton nightie. She plopped down on her back in bed and stared at the ceiling in the dark.

First thing tomorrow she'd call him.

Oh, joy. Something to look forward to. A conference with the evil twin.

Two days after the auction, Jake waded through a dozen voice mails at his office at Hellfire, International, hating it that he wasn't on-site with his men.

"You get caught up in another fire," his doctor had warned him before he'd released him from the hospital after his accident, "and the next time you won't walk away. The damage to your lungs is just too extensive to risk it. They can't take another hit."

Sidelined. Jake hated it. To take his mind off the reality that ate at him every day, he started thinking about the auction again. He wasn't sure why he'd done it. Not just that he'd gotten ornery and outbid Chrissie Travers for the box of junk, but why he'd told her he'd give her the stuff if she'd go with him to the ball.

Now, where in the name of anything sane had that come from? Okay. Sanity probably hadn't had anything to do with it. Sheer impulse had.

Still, that didn't explain why he'd asked her. Probably because he'd figured she'd do exactly what she'd done—stick that little nose of hers high in the air and turn him down flat.

He glanced at the box he'd brought to work and set on the floor in the corner. It was as closed up and secretive as the prickly Ms. Travers.

"Let's just call it a testosterone moment," he muttered grimly and leaned back in his leather chair. For some inexplicable reason, the woman was always messing with his hormones. And that in itself was a major puzzle.

She was so not his type. Uppity little tight-ass. That's what she was. He'd always gone more for the party girls who wanted to have a good time, knew how to have a good time and didn't beat themselves up the next morning after they'd had a good time. Prissy Chrissie wouldn't know a good time if it sneaked up and bit her on her cute, curvy butt.

So why did he find himself grinning at the prospect

of seeing her again? And why did he have this recurring fantasy of biting the cute little butt in question?

Uncomfortable with his turn of thoughts, he sobered and stood abruptly, tucking the tips of his fingers into the back pockets of his jeans. He walked to the window of his fourth-floor office and stared down at the street.

Well, well, well, he thought, feeling a little too much pleasure when he saw who was walking down the street. Speak of the devil—or in this case, the saint. There she was. Little Miss Priss, in all her starched-panties glory.

He leaned a shoulder against the window frame, crossed his arms over his chest and looked his fill as she marched down the sidewalk toward his building. All she needed was a uniform and she could be captain of a drill team.

What made a woman, he wondered and reached up to scratch his jaw, who was put together in a package like a sweet little china doll think she had to go through life like a caricature of a turn-of-the-century, stiff-backed, prim and proper suffragette?

Hell, he bet she *did* starch her panties. And they were probably white. Most likely cotton. With days of the week that she always wore on the proper day.

Why that image made him hot, he had no idea.

She was within a block now and he couldn't help but appreciate the view. She was barely five-four. Her pale blond hair and large hazel eyes gave her a cute, fragile, elfin look that in his weaker moments made him want to protect her as much as provoke her. Since he was fairly certain she'd never let anyone protect her—regardless that she looked as delicate as the petals on a yellow rose—provoking her was a much better bet.

And again, she was not his type. She was the exact opposite of Rea, who'd been svelte, sexy and as predatory as a jungle cat. Thoughts of his ex made him shiver. Too bad he'd been so blinded by the svelte, sexy parts that he'd missed the other characteristic until it was too late.

Whoa, what's this, he wondered when he saw Chrissie cross the street. Without a doubt she was on her way up to see him.

Fine. He walked away from the window, picked up the box and set it on his desk. He'd been about to have his secretary call a courier to pick it up and deliver it to Chrissie anyway. This would save him a buck or two. He'd had his fun. Now she could have her precious box. And the musty-smelling saddlebag that was in it.

His secretary, Janice Smith, who had been with him from the beginning seven years ago, buzzed him on the intercom as he settled in behind his desk.

"Yes, Janice."

"Christine Travers is here to see you, Mr. Thorne."

"Send her in."

He rocked back in his chair. Propping his elbows on the arms and steepling his fingers beneath his chin, he prepared to be magnanimous. It wasn't nearly as much fun as being obnoxious, but, hey, if nothing else, it would be a kick to throw her off guard by being nice.

* * *

She should have called, Christine realized when she found herself standing outside Jacob Thorne's office door. Her palms began to sweat. She should have saved herself the stress of a face-to-face meeting.

But that was the coward's way out and she'd never been that. She wasn't starting now. Not for someone like him.

She turned the handle and stepped inside, expecting...well, not really knowing what to expect when she entered his inner sanctum. He did, however, manage to surprise her.

The office was large but not ostentatious. The furniture was top-of-the-line but functional, all stylish black lacquer and shining chrome. There wasn't a dead animal in sight—either on the floor made into a rug or on the wall in the guise of a hat rack or displayed as a trophy. She grudgingly gave him points for that. And for the stunning collection of photographs adorning the walls.

Each dramatically framed photo was of a different oil fire site. And each photo captured all the fury, the danger and the unyielding hunger of the flames shooting into the air like geysers and of the courageous men who risked their lives putting them out.

"Impressive, aren't they?"

She jerked her attention from the photographs to the man lounging idly behind a desk that was far from empty yet neat and uncluttered. He was watching her with a look that made her think of a lion lounging lazily in the sun, overseeing the lioness doing all the work.

Clearly, though, he was a hands-on boss if the stacks of paperwork were any indication. Okay. So he got another point for being involved.

"Very," she agreed belatedly with a nod back to the photos, because what was really impressive was the way he looked behind that desk and she didn't want him to see how he had affected her. Since her cheeks were hot, she figured they were also pink. It was a curse of her fair complexion.

In the meantime she'd never seen him in business mode. She'd seen him at death's door, as pale as the hospital sheets beneath him. She'd seen him all sexy swagger and irritating indolence, as he'd been the other night at the auction. This man-in-charge persona was disconcerting—and unexpectedly appealing.

His shirt was white. The top button was undone and his cuffs were rolled up on his strong forearms. His brown suit jacket and a truly stunning silk tie hung on the coatrack behind him. Style. He had it. In spades.

"That one was taken in Kuwait," he said when she averted her attention to a print that, once she was able to study it without being hyperaware of him, gave her chills just thinking about the fierceness of the blaze.

"I'll go to the ball with you," she said without turning back to him.

Okay. It was out. She hadn't intended to just blurt it out that way but now that she was here, now that she was suddenly aware of him as an entity other than the proverbial Thorne-in-her-side, she wanted to get this over with and get away from him as quickly as possible. And away from this unbelievable resurgence of attraction that not only blindsided her but also shook her composure. The sooner they cut this deal, the sooner she could go on about her business.

When she was met with nothing but silence, she drew a bracing breath and turned toward him.

He was frowning. Not a gloating or even an angry frown, but more as though he was in deep thought or contemplating something heavy.

"I said I'd go to the ball with you," she repeated, and he finally rocked forward in his chair and came to attention behind his desk.

"So you did."

And still he scowled.

Perplexed, she eyed him with wary suspicion. "Wasn't that the condition?"

"Of me turning over the box?"

Her exasperation at the way he was drawing this out came in the form of an impatient breath. "I believe it was."

"Ah. Well, you just said the magic word. Was. That *was* my condition. Two days ago. But *now,* we're dealing with today."

She narrowed her eyes. "There was a time limit?"

"It seems so, yeah."

Sure. *Now* he was smiling.

Because this was still a joke to him. He had never intended for her to go to the dance with him. Just as she'd thought. He'd merely been playing with her, and when she'd called him on it, he'd figured a way to weasel out of the invitation. It shouldn't have hurt so much.

"Why is this stuff so important to you anyway?" he asked, standing. He walked around the desk and settled a hip on its corner.

"Historic value," she said truthfully.

He crossed his arms over his chest and scowled. "Musty saddlebags? Old guns? A lady's purse? What else? Oh, yeah. A faded map."

Her heart jumped over itself. "You looked?"

"You may have heard. It's *my* box. I'm pretty sure that means I'm entitled to look."

This was going nowhere. And she'd had enough of his fun and games. She'd figure out another way to get the box of Jess Golden's things to the Historical Society. Maybe she could get some of the city matriarch types to put a little heat on him or something.

"Sorry to have taken your time," she said and headed for the door.

"Wait. Wait. You haven't heard the new condition."

She stopped, her hand on the door handle, and let out a deep breath. Knowing she was going to regret this, she turned and met his smug smile. "New condition?"

He pushed off the desk. "Tell you what. Let's talk about it over lunch."

"Lunch?"

He reached around her to open the door. "You know. The light meal between breakfast and dinner?"

"But—"

"I'll be back in an hour or so, Janice," he said, herding Christine out of his office and into the reception area with a hand at the small of her back. "Anybody calls, tell 'em I'll get back to them—unless it's Ray. If Ray calls, tell him to phone my cell."

Christine was far too aware of his hand touching her there, ever so lightly at the small of her back. "I'm not going to lunch with you."

"Oh, lighten up, Chrissie, would you? It's noon. I'm hungry. I figure you're hungry, too. It's that simple. It's not like it's a date or anything."

She told herself his last statement didn't sting. And it wouldn't have—at least not so badly—if Janice, stylish and chic in her tailored white blouse and short red skirt, hadn't glanced up and cast Christine a sympathetic look when they passed the desk.

He'd just made it clear to anyone within earshot that Jacob Thorne didn't consider Christine Travers datable.

Which was perfectly fine. She lifted her chin. She didn't want to date him anyway. And she didn't want to go to lunch with him. What she wanted was to get as far away from the reproachable evil twin as she could, considering they lived in the same city.

And that was the truth.

Three

Okay. Jake had surprised himself again. He simply had been going to give Chrissie the box. End of story. So what had happened to the plan?

Why was he sitting across from her in a booth at the Royal Diner happy as a damn clam because little Chrissie looked all pouty and put out?

As usual the diner was packed. It never seemed to matter that the greasy spoon, with its smoke-stained walls, cracked bar stools and chipped countertops, had seen better days. The place stayed popular with the locals for two basic reasons: nobody knew their way around a grill like Manny Hernandez and nobody gave lip like the mainstay waitress, Sheila Foster. A lot of guys came in just to let Sheila rag on them. Himself included.

Montgomery and Gentry belted out a song from the beat-up jukebox as Jake watched Chrissie pick at one of Manny's burger baskets with all the enthusiasm of a *Fear Factor* competitor contemplating eating a box of scorpions.

"You don't like the burger?"

"Do you know how much fat is in one of these things?" she grumbled.

"So why did you order it?"

"I didn't. *You* did. I wanted a salad and you said I was too thin and why didn't I eat something with some substance. So I said fine, I'll have what you're having."

"Oh, yeah." He grinned. "I forgot."

Actually he hadn't forgotten anything. He'd wanted to see her eat something that he figured she would consider sinful. And then he wanted to watch the lady enjoy sinning. Wait until she saw the pecan pie with ice cream that followed his standing lunch order.

He didn't know why but he was suddenly determined to loosen her up and make her enjoy herself in spite of her determination not to. Not, he told himself, because he particularly cared, but because sometime during the course of this day—okay, if he were being honest, it was long before today—she had started to become a personal challenge to him.

People liked him. Pretty much without exception.

Chrissie Travers was the major dissenter. For whatever reason, he wanted to change that.

As a rule, folks liked his teasing. They liked his sense of humor. They liked that he thought life should be lived to the fullest whenever possible because so much in these times was tough to deal with. And they liked that he knew about tough from the trenches. Just as he knew what it was like to face down death and come out on top.

A near-death experience like he'd had five years ago had a tendency to change a man's outlook on life—it had sure as the world prompted him to want to live the rest of it on terms of his own making. Terms that included squeezing out as much pleasure as possible. Unlike the super-duper-serious Christine Travers, who was his polar opposite when it came to pursuing fun.

So he'd pulled a squeeze play on Chrissie, who really wasn't too thin or all that difficult to squeeze. He'd said she was thin to get her riled again and see the color rise in her cheeks because she looked so pretty in pink. In fact, despite her spinster-slash-warden suits, which ranged in color from navy blue to black to—God save her—dirt brown, she looked kinda cute just the way she was. Well, cute except for the sourpuss attitude that was going to give her wrinkles before she turned thirty.

The woman was a puzzle. Flat out. And he did love a puzzle. Which probably explained why he kept trying to fit the pieces together.

"So. Tell me," he said, digging into his own burger, "what do you do for fun?"

She blinked at him as if she didn't understand the question. "Fun?"

He shook his head, swallowed and wiped his mouth with a paper napkin. "I'm sensing a severe shortfall in your basic vocabulary here. *Lunch. Fun.* Do I dare introduce the word *play?*"

The woman had some expressions. Most of them pinched—as if she was sitting on something prickly and was too polite to take care of the problem in public. *What would people think?*

He wondered what it was going to take to make her smile. He'd given it a halfhearted effort for five years now and so far he hadn't hit the magic word, number or combination. Maybe it was time he got serious.

"I thought we were going to talk about your new conditions."

"Fine. Right. We are." He bit into his burger and chewed thoughtfully. "First tell me why—no smoke screen this time—that stuff is so important to you."

She considered him across her uneaten burger and fries. Instead of answering, she asked a question. "You're a Texas Cattleman's Club member, right?"

"Right," he said, popping a fry into his mouth and letting her play this out.

"And Cattleman's Club members are sworn to certain values. Like loyalty and trust and honor and all that, right?"

He nodded and leaned back on the faded gray vinyl booth, wondering where this was going.

"Then if I tell you something in confidence—something that could affect Royal's future—you're sworn to secrecy, correct?"

He matched her pinched-brow scowl. "Absolutely. Of course, to make certain there's no breach in that confidence, we're both going to have to swear it in blood. You got a pocketknife on ya?"

She let out a disgusted little huff. "Do you take anything seriously?"

"Not if I can help it. Now, for Pete's sake, spit it out. If you want me to keep it on the QT, all you have to do is ask."

"Well, I'm asking," she said, so sober it was all he could do not to laugh.

"Okay. Consider it done. Now give."

"You know the Jessamine Golden legend?"

"Some of it," he said. If you grew up in Royal, you'd heard about Jessamine Golden. It was as staple a part of the town's history as the feud between two prominent families, the Windcrofts and the Devlins. "She was an outlaw, right? Killed the mayor and the sheriff. Stole some gold. Let's see…disappeared somewhere around the early 1900s."

"Right. Okay. Well…the saddlebags?" She leaned in close and lowered her voice.

"Yes?" he said, doing the same. Mostly because it got him a little closer to her and he'd been wondering if that really was gold shot through her pretty hazel eyes. Not only gold but silver, he realized. *So that's what gives them that iridescent color.*

And didn't she have the longest, most lush eyelashes he'd ever seen? Soft as sable, thick as a paintbrush. Why hadn't he ever noticed that before?

Or her freckles. Cute little angel kisses lightly dusted the rise of her cheekbones and skimmed the bridge of her pixie nose. He was surprised he'd never noticed them before, either. Of course, he'd never been this close. Kissing close, if he were of a notion to steal one, which he might be if he didn't have a pretty good idea of how she'd react. Those even pearly whites of hers would probably rip into his lip like tiger teeth.

"I'm sure," she said, and he was mesmerized by the mobility of her full lips, "that those saddlebags belonged to Jess Golden."

"Where did you get that?" he asked, frowning suddenly when he noticed a very fine, very faint crescent line of a scar at the bottommost edge of her pointed chin. It was about an inch long, and of course he'd never noticed it before, either. That close factor again.

She pulled back, looking exasperated. "Where did I get what?"

"That scar," he said, reaching across the battered gray Formica tabletop and gently pinching her chin between his thumb and index finger so he could angle her head for a better look. And on second look, it wasn't so fine and it wasn't so faint. "Man. That had to have hurt like blazes."

"We were talking about the saddlebags," she said,

pulling away from his hold and touching her fingers to her chin in a gesture that was both self-conscious and embarrassed.

Okay. The scar was a sore subject. So he let it drop. For now. But after five years of dancing around the edge of her fire, he seriously wanted to know what fueled her flames. He could be patient when the need arose. "What about the saddlebags?"

"I said I'm certain they belonged to Jess Golden."

He sat back. Shrugged. "What makes you think so?"

She went into an excited diatribe about Jess Golden once living in Jonathan Devlin's house, about the purse and the rose petals and the six-shooters and the map coming from Jonathan's attic. And there was that pink blush on her cheeks again. So. Anger and excitement were two of her triggers. He wondered what else got her going and flashed on an image of her face flushed with the heat of great sex.

Whoa.

That was interesting. And the picture was a little too vivid.

"The roses are a dead giveaway," she finished.

"Hmm. Roses, huh? An outlaw who liked roses?"

"I have always figured there was more to Jess Golden than what was written in the local newspapers at the time and recorded in local history books."

He considered her and realized she'd finally revealed a chink in that airtight armor. "Well, well, well, Chrissie. *You've* got a romantic streak."

She blinked several times in rapid succession, clearly flustered. "I am not a romantic."

"You've romanticized an outlaw," he pointed out.

"Romanticized? That's ridiculous." She blushed again, as if the notion that he might think that she— Christine Travers of the straitlaced, all work, no play variety—would have any thought on the subject of romance was too absurd to consider. Or because he was right and she really was a closet romantic.

Huh. *Who'da thunk it?* And on the heels of that discovery, possibilities abounded. How hard would it be to romance this standoffish little blonde? How soft would she be when she let some of the starch out of her spine?

"The point is," she pressed on, "if I'm right and those are Jess Golden's things, the map could lead to the stolen gold."

"Okay. Hold it. If those are her things, what makes you think the gold is still here? Why wouldn't she have taken it with her?"

She gave him a "duh" look and evidently decided he needed remedial training. "You're an outlaw," she began as if she was talking to a five-year-old.

He leaned back, held both hands up, palms out. "Swear to God, I did not steal that gold."

Nothing. Not even a smirk. And he wanted to pry one out of her so badly.

"I didn't mean that you are an outlaw literally," she said, enunciating each word, again as if she were talking to someone who was intellectually challenged. "I meant, you're an outlaw hypothetically. And you're on the run because everyone in Texas believes you killed not only the mayor of the town but the sheriff, as well. You stole the gold and don't have the time or the means to take it with you. It's heavy and cumbersome. So you hide it. And you draw a map. You hide the map somewhere—like in the house where you live, in the attic or something—and then you run, hoping things will settle down after a time and you can go back and get it."

"Okay," he said, marginally intrigued now. "I'm an outlaw—well, not me specifically, because we're still doing hypothetical, right?"

Only a card-carrying optimist could interpret her sneer as camouflage for a grin.

"What makes you think that I—the hypothetical outlaw—didn't come back and dig up the gold later?"

"Because there are absolutely no accounts of Jess Golden ever being spotted in or around Royal again. Ever. And the gold was in the form of numbered bars. If they'd been converted to cash, there would be a record. There's not. I checked."

She was thorough. He'd give her that. And he'd give her something else. She hid it well, but there was a treasure trove of pent-up passion buried beneath the layers that comprised Chrissie Travers. At least she had passion about this issue. He suspected there might be something else that would fire her up and toyed with the idea of being the man to discover exactly what that something was.

The prospect of peeling those layers and discovering,

little by little, the woman hiding behind the steel facade suddenly fascinated him. For years he'd found a certain sophomoric satisfaction in simply pulling her chain, then leaving her stewing in her own juices.

He didn't feel so much like leaving now. Instead he felt as if maybe he owed it to her to help her come out of her cocoon. Yeah, he thought, warming to the idea. And maybe he owed it to himself to see whether a butterfly or a bug wiggled its way out.

"Tell you what," he said, putting his money on the butterfly. "Since you've made such a compelling argument—" he reached for the ketchup bottle and dumped a generous glob on top of her uneaten French fries "—I think you deserve to have the box."

"But?"

He smiled at her insight and helped himself to some of her fries. "But there are still conditions."

He was getting a little addicted to that icy glare. He didn't know anyone who did it so well. He swiped a few more fries. "Condition number one—you eat at least half of your burger and some of the fries."

"This is ridiculous."

"Pretty minor, really."

She leaned back in the booth, her head tilted with both impatience and irritation. "What do you want from me? Why do you take such pleasure in baiting me?"

"Well, to tell you the truth, I didn't have a clear answer to that question myself until a few minutes ago."

"And what happened to clear things up?"

"I think it's the freckles," he said happily and watched her eyes shift from irritation to confusion to flat-out exasperation. "They're cute. And so are you. Now eat your lunch and then we'll lay out the rest of the terms."

"And one of the conditions is a dinner date?" Alison asked later that evening. She sounded just a little too cheery to suit Christine.

Actually Jacob never did get around to talking about terms. He'd said they would discuss them over dinner. Which was not a date.

"A dinner *meeting*," Christine clarified. "Saturday night."

She still couldn't believe she'd agreed to it. Not only that, she didn't want to believe it. The man was devious and manipulative and…and he thought she was cute. Right. As if she believed that.

"What do you suppose he's really after?" she asked Alison as they sat side by side on Christine's sofa, wearing their sweats, a popcorn bowl between them, their stocking feet propped on the coffee table as the opening credits to the movie Alison had chosen for their traditional "Wednesday night at the movies" rolled by.

"What's he after? Sweetie, I've been trying to tell you. He's after *you*," Alison said, grabbing a pillow and hugging it to her chest. "This is a tearjerker," she added offhandedly as if she hadn't just made the most ridiculous statement of the year.

"He is *not* after me," Christine insisted and dug into the popcorn.

"So why did he fabricate yet another excuse to see you in the guise of leveling conditions on giving you Jess Golden's things? No man goes to those lengths to tease a woman unless it's because he's interested in her."

There was no convincing Alison otherwise, so Christine let it drop. She watched the movie. And told herself Alison was all wet. Jacob Thorne was not interested in her. It didn't make any sense that he would be. A man like him. A woman like her. Talk about oil and water.

"So. Where are you two going on your second date?"

"It's not a date," Christine insisted. "And where do you get second?"

"Who paid for lunch?"

"Well, he did but—"

"Then it's a second date. Now, where are you going?"

"Claire's," she finally confessed.

"Oh là là! Big-time date."

Christine only grunted. She'd never been to Royal's swanky French restaurant. Claire's wasn't exactly in her everyday budget. Or even in her special-occasion budget, for that matter. And while she wasn't looking forward to spending an evening—that was *not* a date— in Thorne's company, she couldn't help but be excited about getting a little taste of how the upper crust lived.

"What are you going to wear?"

Christine shrugged and feigned interest in the movie.

"I hadn't really thought about it." Okay. That was a lie. It's all she'd thought about. "Probably my black pantsuit."

Alison sat up straight. "Eeewwww. You can't go to Claire's in that boxy old thing."

"What do you mean, old thing? It's only—" She stopped and thought. Hmm. It had been a long time since she'd bought the suit.

"Tomorrow we're going shopping during our lunch hour," Alison said. "And you're going to buy something sexy."

"I am not."

"Are, too."

"I. Am. Not."

"We'll see," Alison said. "Now let's watch the movie. I'm due for a good cry."

The dress was black. And short. And low cut.

The heels were silver. And spiked. And strappy. And they showed off siren-red toenail polish that Alison had insisted was perfect for the total look.

She had a look, all right, Christine thought, hovering just one notch to the left of panicked on Saturday night. A look she'd never in a million years thought she could pull off. Yet as she took it all in—experiencing a mixture of disbelief and shock and a pleasurable womanly confidence—in her full-length bedroom mirror, Christine had to admit Alison was right.

She looked hot.

"Okay. That settles it. I'm changing."

Alison laughed. "Don't even think about it," she said, standing behind her like a drill sergeant.

Right. She'd forgotten about Alison for a minute there. Her friend had insisted she help Christine get ready for her dinner *meeting* and then informed her she was going to stick around until Jacob arrived just to make sure she didn't chicken out and ditch the new duds for the black pantsuit.

"Alison, I look ridiculous."

"You look fabulous."

"I look obvious."

"I really like the hair, too," Alison added, ignoring Christine's discomfort.

Yeah. Christine had to admit Alison was right about that, too. Her hair did look great. Alison had scooped it up to the crown of her head and wrestled it into a spiky little puff that looked chic and hip and—yeah, she admitted, still amazed—sexy.

It was a word that had never fit her.

Conservative—now, there was a word she wore well. A word that was comfortable, unlike the way she felt wearing this dress. She *had* to change clothes. Desperate times called for desperate measures.

"Okay. Thank you, thank you, thank you for everything. You've transformed the pumpkin into a fancy coach, Fairy Godmother. You must be exhausted. Why don't you go on home now?"

"Yeah, right," Alison said. "And give you a chance

to change into something less revealing, less sexy and more conservative the minute I walk out the door? Uh-uh. Besides, it's too late. Mr. Wonderful just pulled up."

Well, yikes, Christine thought and tugged up the plunging neckline in a vain attempt to cover a little more skin.

"Go," Alison said and gave her an encouraging squeeze. "Answer the door. And let the begging begin."

Yeah. As if Jacob Thorne would ever beg for her.

On a deep breath she walked out of the bedroom. Her knees were wobbly as she headed down the hall and regarded the front door to her apartment as if Jack the Ripper were about to make an impromptu appearance.

Not Jack. Jacob. Jacob the Thorne. And his knock was solid and confident.

She wished she could say the same about her knees. This was so ridiculous. The way she looked. The way she'd dressed. The outrageous way her heart was hammering. All because the man on the other side of the door had orchestrated a pretend date to have a little more fun at her expense.

The reminder was all she needed to regain her composure. He wanted to make a joke of her? Fine. At least she was turned out in a way that might give him a twinge of regret.

She wiped her sweaty palms on her skirt and immediately regretted that she may have soiled the delicate silk crepe. Regrouping, she pasted on a smile and opened the door.

"Hi," she said and had the disarming experience of watching his arrogant hey-baby grin slowly deflate to be replaced by a look of complete and utter shock.

Four

"**U**m…hello?" Christine repeated again after several long, uncomfortable seconds had passed.

He hadn't said a word. He just stood there. Looking her up and down. Slowly. Very slowly.

"Hello," he said finally, his voice deep and gruff. Very, very gruff. "Hello, hello, hello," he repeated slowly.

His smile had returned. A pleased, surprised, uniquely charming smile, and if she wasn't careful, she might start to think he actually was happy to see her. And that he actually liked what he saw.

"You have legs," he said, standing back to take another long, blatantly appreciative look. "Nice legs."

"Um. Well."

Sparkling response, Christine. Just sparkling.

"Nice, Chrissie," he said, meeting her eyes again. "You look very, very nice."

"Um. Well."

Is there a really stupid echo in here? And why are my cheeks so hot?

"I'll…I'll, um, just go get my purse."

"It will be my pleasure to wait here and watch you go get it," he said, another grin in his voice that made her glance back over her shoulder—and get caught off guard by the heated look in his eye.

She turned her head back so fast, she made herself dizzy. At least, that's why she thought she was dizzy. It had nothing to do with the way he looked in his rich cobalt-blue suit and expertly knotted silk tie. Or the way he smelled—like some pricey, seductive, masculine cologne that brought to mind mint and musk and the subtle undercurrents of testosterone.

And it definitely had nothing to do with the way he was looking at her. As if he wanted to gobble her up in one big, wolfish bite.

Wolfish? Get real. This wolf usually hunted for foxier game than her. He probably had indigestion or something.

She felt a hot river of self-consciousness trickle through her. Why was she putting herself through this? Maybe he did like what he saw—but what he saw was an illusion. A surprise in something other than drab mode.

She was still exactly what Jacob Thorne thought she

was—a dowdy, inexperienced, pushing-thirty old maid trying to play dress-up. A woman who was so afraid of men because of what her father had done to her and her mother and so afraid of letting herself fall into that same horrible spiral of humiliation and pain that her M.O. was to make herself as plain and unappealing as possible so men wouldn't notice her. And God forbid a man ever showed any interest in her, because she'd pop out her porcupine quills and warn him away with her bristles and barbs.

She felt chilled to the bone suddenly. And hot all over at the same time. Talk about self-discovery. Why did she have to experience this particular discovery now? And why did it have tears gathering in her throat?

"Chris?"

She turned her head to see Alison standing in the bedroom doorway holding her purse. The concern in her eyes had Christine blinking back tears again.

"Oh, sweetie. What's wrong?"

"I can't do this," she whispered. "I'm not the kind of woman who can go out to dinner with that kind of man."

"The hell you can't," Alison said, intuitively sensing that Christine was in the midst of a monumental cold-feet moment. "Don't you dare put yourself down that way."

Alison shoved the little black clutch purse into Christine's hand. "Now, you are not going to waste that dress and that hair and that makeup, do you understand me? You. Look. Incredible. Work it. Enjoy it. Feel the power, girl. You own it tonight. And the way you look, you're gonna own him, too."

Alison hugged her hard, then turned her around and literally shoved her into the hall.

"There you are," her date said when she lurched into the living room. "Thought you'd decided to bail on me."

Alison's words bounced around in her head.

Feel the power. You own it....

As incredible as it seemed, when she looked and saw real interest—not just surprised curiosity—in Jacob's eye, she did feel the power. At least, a little power surge. For all of his smooth words and sexy smiles, she'd never seen him quite the way he was tonight.

Off balance. Just a tad uncertain. As though maybe he really did like what he saw—and it had surprised him.

Maybe the balance of power *had* shifted in that moment when she'd opened her door and he'd seen her standing there. Not looking like Prissy Chrissie Travers, as even she had begun to think of herself. But looking like a woman. A vibrant, self-confident woman who recognized her burgeoning power—yes, power—over a man who had always had the upper hand.

Okay. Maybe that was overplaying it. But there was something. If not power, at least a measure of self-confidence she'd never felt before. With luck, it would last through the evening.

"Bail? No," she said as a calm resolve descended over her. "I'm not going to bail."

The stakes were suddenly too high. This was no longer just about acquiring Jess Golden's things. This was about something bigger. Much bigger. And as soon as she figured out exactly what was happening to shake her and yet empower her, she'd know what she wanted to do about it.

Butterfly, Jake thought as they walked into Claire's and he got a whiff of some exotic, flowery perfume. She'd definitely turned into a butterfly. Sleek, satiny and mysterious. And, man, had it been worth the hassle to witness the full effect of the metamorphosis.

Superserious, profoundly professional and supremely prickly Christine Travers with her sensible clothes and plain-Jane package was long gone. In her place was a sophisticated, sexy siren possessed of an underlying vulnerability that sent his heart rate rocketing.

He liked it. He liked it a lot. And he was starting to think that maybe she might be a woman he could like a lot, too. Not that he hadn't always liked her, it was simply that the dynamics of their relationship had changed drastically when he'd invited her to dinner. He was used to prickly Chrissie. Had taken great pains to bring out that side of her.

Now he was faced with sexy Chrissie—a side of her he'd always known existed if she would just let her come out and play. Yet for some reason this new face made him a little nervous—which was nuts because he was never nervous around women.

She'd done something amazing to her hair. Not that he didn't think it looked cute when she wore it down and straight and framing her pixie face in a businesslike do. It was just that with all that fine blond mass swept up on top of her head...well, it had an effect, was all. It accentuated the model-slim line of her neck and exposed a delectable-looking nape. A nape that tempted him mightily to bend down and place a kiss there when she sat at the table for two he'd reserved and he pushed the chair in for her.

He caved in to a spike of better judgment and had to satisfy himself with wondering how badly him kissing her there would rattle her as he settled across the table from her.

"Good evening, Mr. Thorne."

Jake smiled at their waiter, Claude Jacques, as he produced open menus. "Hello, Claude. How's it going?"

"Superb, thank you. Would you and the lady care for something to drink while you decide on dinner?"

"Chrissie?" Jake said over the top of his menu. "Would you like something? The wine selection is excellent."

"I think I'd prefer a club soda, thanks. With a lime wedge, please," she added with a flash of her gray-green eyes at Claude before she went back to studying her menu.

"Make it two," Jake said, deferring to her choice, although he'd have loved to see the color a little wine would have splashed on her cheeks.

Not that she needed color. She was...hell...glowing? Close enough. Her lips shimmered with color—

somewhere between a wine-red and hot-pink. And he had another I-never-noticed-that-before moment. He'd never noticed that her lips were so full, so lush, and they looked so kissably soft.

He missed the freckles, though. She'd camouflaged them with some powder or blush or bronzer or Lord knew what little bit of magic she'd pulled out of her woman's bag of tricks.

Speaking of magic, the dress was the mother of all illusions. It had been driving him crazy since she'd opened her apartment door and magically drained all the blood from his head and shot it directly to his groin. He was a sucker for black, short and plunging necklines. All that pale, creamy skin against and beneath the black silk was a turn-on of epic proportions.

"Did I mention that you look incredible?" he said, watching her studiously avoid eye contact by gluing her gaze to the menu.

Several beats passed before she lowered the menu and met his eyes. "You did, actually. Or words to that effect. Thank you. You, um, you look very nice, as well."

Aren't we formal now? Again he thought it was cute. So was the way her gaze sort of lingered involuntarily on his mouth before sliding to his chest, then gliding slowly back to his mouth again.

"So, do you see anything you like?"

Her gaze snapped to his.

"On the menu," he clarified with a grin.

There was that blush. The one he loved to fire up. The

one that told him that she hadn't been thinking about food when she'd been checking him out but that there might have been hunger involved and that it embarrassed her to be caught whetting her appetite, so to speak.

"I'm not too knowledgeable on French cuisine," she said, sounding self-conscious.

"That's what Claude's for," he said, wanting to set her at ease. "Let's ask him what's good when he brings our drinks."

He watched with interest when she did just that, leading the waiter through a series of questions, both polite and businesslike in manner, until she finally settled on whitefish in wine sauce.

"Make mine beef, make it red and make it big," he said when it was his turn. "And I'll have whatever the lady's having for side dishes."

"You will enjoy." Claude scooped up the menus. "The lady has excellent taste."

And then they were alone. If you didn't count the discreetly hovering army of wait staff—one who placed ice in their water glasses with sterling tongs, another who dropped in a wedge of lemon and yet another who finally got to the task of pouring the water.

Her expressive eyes relayed her amazement over all the fuss about filling a water glass.

"Not exactly the Royal Diner, huh?"

"Not exactly."

"It's a little pretentious," he agreed, "but the food's great."

"It's a beautiful place."

Ritzy is what it was. Valet parking, white linen table-cloths, red roses in crystal vases on every table. Women liked it. Besides the great food, the part he liked was the candlelight—something he'd never really paid much attention to before tonight.

Tonight the lighting seemed the perfect accompaniment to the woman sharing his table. It also played into a little fantasy that had been growing in size and scope since the blonde in black had opened her door and rocked his world.

He'd been anticipating staid, stodgy and subdued. The last thing he'd expected was sexy with a capital SEX. And again he felt that niggling sense of unease that he wanted to discount as nothing more than pleasant surprise. Oh, yeah. Had she ever surprised him.

"Are you having a good time?"

"Is that what this is about? Me having a good time?"

It didn't take much to put her on the defensive. His fault. He'd done little more than give her grief for five years. He wasn't even sure why he'd changed the game plan now. "Well, I would hope so. What did you want it to be about?"

"Jess Golden's things."

"Ah. But I don't want to talk about that yet."

A frown brimming with rebuke crinkled up her forehead.

"Later," he promised. "I want to talk about you first."

Clearly she hadn't been prepared for that.

"Jacob—" she began to say, a clear preamble to another roadblock.

"Jake," he interrupted. "My friends call me Jake. And for once don't argue, okay? Let's enjoy the evening."

He sat back in his chair, toyed with the stem of his water glass and watched her face. It didn't hide her emotions nearly as well as it hid her secrets. She was uncomfortable. It was one thing for him to put her on edge with a little good-natured teasing. It was another for her to feel discomfort because she thought she was out of her element, which is what he suspected was going on right now. And he wanted to remedy that situation ASAP. "How about we start with something easy? Do you like your work?"

"I do. Yes," she said without hesitation—and with a noticeable lack of elaboration.

Okay. So he was going to have to pry every snippet of information out of her. "Why a respiratory therapist? And yes," he insisted at her doubtful look, "I really am interested."

"My freshman year of college," she said at long last, "I was awarded some work-study money. My assignment was at the university hospitals and clinics. Cleaning rooms, if you really want to know. I rotated between several floors and got interested in respiratory therapy when I was working in that unit."

"Work-study? So you worked your way through school?"

"Pretty much, yes."

"What other types of jobs did you have?"

Their bread came about that time, so she busied her hands with it and seemed to let down her guard a little in the process. "Too many to count. Let's see...I tended bar, worked the night shift at the front desk of a couple of motels, cashiered at a convenience store. Whatever it took to make tuition and board."

His admiration for her kicked up a couple more notches. "Sounds tough."

She shook her head, not an ounce of regret registering on her face. "Sometimes, yes, but for the most part I enjoyed it all. Appreciated every job I had. Without them, I wouldn't have gotten my degree."

"Your family wasn't in a position to help?" He broke off a chunk of bread and picked up his butter knife.

What little reserve she'd let down jumped back up with a vengeance. Instead of answering, she asked her own question. "And what did you study in college? I don't recall ever seeing any courses in oil-well fire-fighting on any course catalogs."

All righty, then. Talking about her family was off-limits. Since she'd struggled to make her own way through college, he had to figure one of two reasons was the cause. Either her family was very poor and she felt self-conscious about it or she was estranged from them, and that just made him more curious about what had precipitated the break.

Regardless, it explained—at least in part—why she was such a serious Sara all the time. She knew hardship.

She knew if not poverty, at least slim pickings. He supposed if he'd had to work as hard as she had to get his education, he'd have a tendency to take life a little more seriously too.

He would have liked to press a little harder about her family, but he took his cues from her and let it drop. "Actually I majored in business management with a minor in accounting."

"Oh, well," she said, buttering a piece of bread, "I can see how that would make a natural transition into fighting oil-well fires."

His smile at her little joke was slow. "So she *does* have a sense of humor."

"When motivated, I can be funny," she said, sounding a little defensive.

"Well, then, I'll have to see what I can do to motivate you more often."

Yeah, he thought when she gave him a wary look. *That means exactly what you think it means. We are going to do this again. This is not a one-time deal, so get used to it, sweetie. I plan to see more of you.*

He wasn't sure when that intention had become apparent to him or why he was so certain he wanted to see more of her. For that matter, he didn't understand the edgy sense of calamity that accompanied his thoughts. He shook it off and rationalized the situation instead. Why did some men find it impossible to resist the lure of Mount Everest? Why did some risk their lives jumping out of planes? Why did he make a living with men who marched into the jaws of oil fires risking everything, including their lives, in the process?

Sometimes the why wasn't nearly as important as the want itself. And right now he wanted to get to know this woman better.

"This bread is delicious."

Nice table talk, but the segue wasn't going to work. "So is the view."

She actually looked behind her to see if she'd missed seeing something. When she turned around and correctly read the look on his face, she didn't exactly roll her eyes, but he could tell she wanted to.

"That was a compliment, Christine."

She set her knife on the edge of her plate, propped her forearms on the table and took his measure. "You don't have to flatter me, Jacob."

He wagged his knife at her. "Jake. And I'm just calling it like I see it."

Oh, that long-suffering look. Oh, that heavy sigh. She was just too much. Was she really that naive?

"You don't really think that tonight is just about Jess Golden's things, do you?"

Now she looked wary again. Maybe not naive. Maybe it was more a question of distrustful. Again. His fault.

"I want to get to know you, Chrissie."

"For what possible reason?"

From any other woman he'd consider the question coy. From her it was exactly what it appeared to be: utter puzzlement.

"I've been giving that some thought." He shrugged. "Maybe because you intrigue me. Maybe because I find you a contradiction. Or maybe because the way you look tonight only increases my curiosity about something that's got me wondering."

She'd grown very still. Even her eyes didn't so much as flicker, although they were wide with the unasked question, *What have you been wondering about?*

"I've been wondering," he said, responding to both the wariness and the anticipation revealed by the accelerated pulse thrumming at the base of her throat, "why you normally go to such lengths to hide the fact that you are a very beautiful woman. And why it embarrasses you to be told that you're beautiful."

"I'm not embarrassed."

Yet she was flushing pink—something he chose not to point out. "What, then?"

"Uncomfortable," she finally said. "I could do without the scrutiny."

He laughed. "Then you shouldn't have worn the dress."

"My thoughts exactly," she grumbled under her breath.

"Okay, look," he said after a moment of her looking as though she wished she was anywhere else but here with anyone else but him, "just lighten up a little. You're taking yourself way too seriously."

"Right. Something you're an expert on."

"Hell, no." He grinned, appreciating her sarcasm. "That's the point. Life's too short to take so dismally serious. You, sweet woman, need a few lessons in loosening up."

"And I suppose you're just the man to teach me."

"There you go. I am definitely the man. And starting tonight, I'm leading the class in the education of Christine Travers, good girl with a yen to go bad."

She smiled. A full-out, bona fide, no-holds-barred smile. Okay. So it was laced with the same sarcasm that sometimes put a bite in her words, but it was a smile. The first one. It felt like a major victory.

"You are so full of it, Thorne," she said, sitting back in her chair when the waiter brought her salad.

"I am, for a fact. Full to bursting with possibilities on how we can loosen you up."

"Not going to happen."

"Because?"

"Because," she said on an exasperated breath, "this is a ridiculous conversation."

He couldn't resist baiting her even more. "Scared?"

Her head snapped up. "Scared? Of what?"

"Of letting go, sweet cheeks. Of living life."

"Just because I'm cautious, just because I'm discriminating, doesn't mean I'm scared. Believe me, I know what scared is…it's something I no longer choose to be. No matter what you think."

Whoa.

I know what scared is…it's something I no longer choose to be.

Her statement shouldn't have come as a surprise, but

it had—to her as well as to him. The expression on her face said she hadn't meant to reveal something so intimate about herself. He hadn't expected the revelation. He'd guessed that there had been some not-so-great events in her life that might have shaped her, contributed to her defensive reserve, but he hadn't wanted to think it was something ugly.

I know what scared is....

Not knowing what she'd endured, only that she had endured it, increased his desire to show her how to have a good time.

"What's the wildest thing you've ever done?" he asked as he dug into his salad. On the other side of the table, she shoved the greens around on her plate. "And don't say it's that you wore your Monday panties on Tuesday 'cause that ain't going to cut it."

He could see that she was a deep breath away from telling him to take his question and put it where the sun don't shine. But reserved, controlled soul that she was, she swallowed back the urge.

"I cut class once," she said.

He grunted in disbelief. "That's it? That's the best you can come up with?"

She shot him a defiant look.

"Oh, Chrissie. Sweetheart. That's pathetic."

"So sue me. I'm a model citizen."

He leaned forward, his fork poised over his salad. "Don't you ever get the urge to be bad? Just do something a little shocking? A little wild?"

Her silence as she finally met his eyes said it all. No. No, she didn't.

"I often work double shifts. I volunteer hours at the Historical Society. I don't have a lot of time left to pursue a sideline of mischief and mayhem. Much like you don't have time out of your fun and games to get involved with something of a little more substance."

"Sticks and stones," he singsonged and pried another reluctant and very small grin out of her.

"You know, there is such a thing as being too frivolous," she pointed out.

"And I would be a prime example?"

"You said it, I didn't."

"So, what if I stepped up to the plate and did something...oh, let's say, civic? You'd consider that a move in the right direction?"

"What direction you move makes no difference to me."

She'd tried to make her words sound snippy but didn't quite accomplish it. She also tried to make him believe it. He didn't.

"I think it does. I think that if I did something—how did you say it? something of substance?—that you might begin to see shades of gray instead of black-and-white and that might prompt you to loosen up a bit."

"It is still beyond me why you care about what I do or think."

"It's a little beyond me, too—or it was until you wore that dress. The fact is, I think we could help each other. I can loosen you up and you can straighten me out."

She patted her mouth with her napkin. "Do you ever quit?"

"No, really, listen. I'm beginning to like this idea." He leaned forward conspiratorially. "How about we make a little deal? I do something you categorize as adult and you do something I categorize as juvenile."

"I'm already doing something juvenile. I'm a party to this conversation."

"You get to pick my project," he pressed on, "and I get to pick yours."

She was about to launch into another protest on the ludicrous content of their conversation—which Jake admitted he'd started and pursued on a lark but now was warming up to—when Gretchen Halifax appeared at their table.

Only his mother's insistence on good manners prompted him to stand and acknowledge her presence.

Five

"Hello, Gretchen," Jake said stiffly when the city councilwoman made it clear she expected an audience. "How are you?"

Gretchen Halifax was not on his list of favorite people. The tall, severe-looking woman with the cold gray eyes and pale blond hair was self-righteous, humorless and demanding. He'd gone toe to toe with her a time or two at city council meetings when she'd refused to see reason and failed to compromise.

"I'm wonderful, Jacob." She smiled, all gleaming white teeth and politician sincerity. She'd perfected that sincerity along with her manipulative ways and somehow had managed to build a large circle of influence in the city.

"I'm sorry to interrupt," she added with barely a glance at Chris, "but I saw you sitting over here and knew I simply must stop by and say hello."

Not on my account, Jake thought but made nice anyway. "Gretchen, this is Chris Travers. Chris, Gretchen Halifax."

With a cool smile Gretchen turned to Chris and extended her hand. "My pleasure, Ms. Travers."

"Gretchen is on the city council," Jake added as Chris extended her hand and said a soft, "Hello."

"Should I know you from somewhere?" Gretchen asked after swiftly appraising Chris.

"I do some volunteer work for the Historical Society," Chris said. "We worked together a couple of times on the Edgar Halifax exhibit."

"Oh, of course. I'm so sorry. Forgive me for not recognizing you. I saw the finished display on Edgar at the museum this afternoon. It's marvelous, don't you think?"

"Display?" Jake asked, not because he was particularly interested in Halifax but because he was interested in Chris's part of it.

"Of my great-great-great-uncle Edgar's historical artifacts," Gretchen explained, oozing self-importance. "It's so exciting that he's been given his rightful place in Royal's history as one of the city's outstanding leaders.

"Edgar was the mayor of Royal in the late 1800s and early 1900s," she added when Jake made an I've-got-no-clue-what-you're-talking-about face.

She beamed while telling the story, making it sound as if old Edgar had come over on the Mayflower.

"Unfortunately Edgar was killed by the outlaw, Jessamine Golden, over a stolen shipment of gold. Speaking of Jessamine Golden, Jake, dear, I heard that you purchased something at the auction the other night that may have belonged to her."

"Where did you hear that?" Chris asked, sounding a little shocked. Clearly she'd hoped to keep the contents of the box between the two of them, Jake thought. At least until he handed it over to her.

"Why, I believe it was your secretary, Jake, who said something to mine over lunch yesterday," Gretchen said, dismissing Chris. "I'd love it if you'd show it to me."

"I can't imagine that you'd be interested in a box of musty old junk."

"Interested? In something that belonged to the woman who killed one of my ancestors? Why, of course I'm interested. Actually I was hoping you'd be willing to part with the items."

"Even if I were, Gretchen, I already have another interested party."

"That's easily solved. I'll double any offer you've got on the table."

He shook his head and from the corner of his eye saw Chrissie's shoulders sag in relief. "If you wanted it so badly, you should have been at the auction and bid on it."

"I would have, but I had a meeting I simply couldn't miss. Okay. I'll triple what you paid for it," Gretchen said, pouncing on him in such a demanding voice, other diners turned to see what was going on.

"Sorry," Jake said, puzzled by Gretchen's almost desperate bid for the box. Even more puzzled about why she was so determined to have Jess Golden's things—if they even were indeed the outlaw's things. "It's not about money."

"Then what would I have to do to get you to part with it?"

He imagined that Gretchen perceived her smile as seductive. He perceived it as predatory. And when she leaned toward him, blatantly inviting him to a view of her cleavage and in effect putting the moves on him without any regard for the fact that his date was watching, he'd had enough. "Give it up, Gretchen. This conversation," he cautioned when he sensed she was about to push a little harder, "is history."

He sat, dismissing her. Gretchen's gray eyes heated in anger, then cooled by slow degrees as she visibly got control of herself. She smiled. Calculated. Tight. And patted her perfectly coiffed hair. Clearly she was not happy that both of her offers had been rejected, but she was determined not to let her anger show.

"Speaking of history," she said, attempting to save face by changing the subject, "I plan to make a little myself. I've officially announced that I'm running for mayor of Royal. Isn't it exciting?"

"Very," Jake said, then covered his obvious lack of excitement with a question. "Who are you running against?"

"At the moment? No one. The incumbent, Maynard Willis, isn't going to run again. Isn't that marvelous?"

Jake shrugged. "Depends on your platform."

"Why, tax reform, of course."

"Tax reform?"

"Specifically as it applies to the oil fields. We've been far too lax in that area—with other local businesses, as well. As a result, we've missed considerable revenue for the city."

The woman was too much. "From where I stand, the local businesses—oil companies included—already are digging pretty deep into their pockets. You get too heavy-handed, they may just decide to relocate to a lower tax base."

"Jacob," she said, as if addressing a rowdy child, "you might want to leave politics to the politicians. All you need to be concerned about," she added with a cheeky smile as she slipped him a business card, "is that a vote for Halifax is a vote for progress."

"Progress my ass," Jake muttered under his breath when she finally walked away.

Christine had listened to—and watched—the exchange between Jacob and Gretchen with interest. Not just because it was a welcome respite from the ridiculous conversation that Jacob—Jake—had insisted on pushing past the limit, but because Gretchen had been so interested in Jess Golden's things. Christine supposed there would be some natural curiosity over items belonging to a woman who had allegedly killed one of her ancestors, but Gretchen had gone a little over the top with her insistence that Jake sell them to her.

Speaking of over the top, could Gretchen have been more obvious making a play for Jake?

The penetrating looks, the subtle brush against him when she'd handed him her card. Christine had seen enough women in action to recognize a come-on when she saw one, even if Gretchen's had been veiled by talk of politics.

Even more amazing than Gretchen making a pass at a guy when he was on a date with another woman was that it hadn't even fazed Jake. He hadn't seemed to care that Gretchen, for all her brassy, fake sincerity and sharp features, was still a very attractive and powerful woman.

"I'm sorry about that," Jake said.

Christine set her salad plate aside. And the words were out before she was aware she'd been thinking them. "Sorry that she was flirting with you?"

He grunted. "Ballsy, huh?"

Took the words right out of her mouth.

"In any event, don't let it bother you. Gretchen flirts with everyone." He scowled at the business card, then tossed it on the table. "As a matter of fact, it's one of the things she does best. Too bad she's not as capable as a city leader."

"So, you wouldn't support her bid for mayor?"

"Hell no. If she gets in, there's no telling what kind of chaos she'll create."

"Because she's a woman?"

"Because she's Gretchen. Whatever gave you the idea that I'm gender biased?"

"Oh, I don't know. Could be the ridiculous conversation we were having earlier."

"Darlin', that wasn't about gender bias. That was about gender equity. I want you to experience some of the fun I have." He waggled his brows. "Show you what it's like to take a little walk on the wild side."

He was incorrigible. And, drat it, he had her smiling again with his silly words. And, yeah, part of the reason she was smiling was because he so clearly was not fazed by Gretchen Halifax's cool sexuality.

Until Gretchen had arrived at the table, Christine had actually started to feel a little less...what? Tense? Self-conscious? Less defensive maybe, despite Jake's questions about her history. She'd even enjoyed his silliness. That had come as a big surprise. Much of this evening had been a surprise—starting with his reaction to seeing her when she'd opened the door. The way he'd looked at her made her feel warm all over, aware, aroused even. And that was the biggest surprise of all.

Their entrées arrived and for a little while they ate in silence. Christine contemplated the way Gretchen had tried to put the moves on Jake. Witnessing Gretchen in action—smooth, sophisticated, worldly—had reminded Christine of one unalterable fact.

While she could enjoy tonight for what it was—one single night—the truth was she wasn't only way out of her element but also was way out of her league. Fancy French restaurants were not on her usual flight path. Men like Jake Thorne moved in privileged circles; she moved in stagnant squares.

She felt let down suddenly. Evidently the power surge sparked by her outfit was officially over. But she decided she was going to make the most of the evening since she'd probably never enjoy the pleasure of Claire's again. With a blissful sigh, she enjoyed a bite of her fish. The wine sauce smothering the whitefish was absolutely decadent.

"Now that's a look you ought to have on your face more often."

She hadn't realized she'd closed her eyes while savoring the rich explosion of flavor saturating her taste buds. "This is delicious."

"And a very sensual experience from where I'm sitting."

She blinked at him, saw the hot appreciation in his gaze and felt herself blush. Again. "How's your steak?"

"Exceptional. And rare. Just the way I like it."

And just the way he liked his women, she figured. There was nothing rare about her. And yet she couldn't quite stall a little shiver of awareness as his gaze swept from her face to her neck, then dropped ever so subtly to the swell of her breasts before he smiled into her eyes.

"Have another bite of your fish. I want to watch you indulge some more."

He'd done it again. Managed to make her face burn with a fire that wasn't fueled as much by irritation as it should have been. Awareness...of him as a man...of herself as a woman, played a bigger part. And it was time to get on top of the situation.

"I think I've waited long enough. It's time to talk about your other condition for turning over Jess Golden's things."

"You haven't been paying attention," he said, that maddeningly amused grin tipping up one corner of his mouth. "I already named it. The condition is we strike a deal. I'll agree to do something you deem as adult and you'll agree to do something I deem as juvenile."

He insisted on pushing. Okay fine. She'd push back. But how?

And just like that, it came to her how she could call his bluff.

"Okay. You're on."

He did a double take. Then sat back in his chair and considered her with a pleasantly disbelieving look. "For real?"

She nodded. "For real."

"Well, okay then, Chris-tine," he said, drawing out her name, "what do I have to do?"

"Run for mayor."

That wiped the smile off his face. "What?"

"You're so confident that Gretchen Halifax will make a lousy candidate? Then you need to make sure she doesn't get the position."

"Hell, sweet cheeks, I'm no politician."

"All the better. You already run a business. It's not much of a stretch to run a city."

"This is ridiculous."

"Oh. *Now* it's ridiculous. Now that I've called you on it."

"But it's my game," he whined with the express intent of making her laugh.

And she did. It just sort of bubbled out, surprising her more than it surprised him.

"Lord, that's sweet," he said. "You really ought to do that more often."

"You make me sound like I'm a stuffy old curmudgeon," she grumbled, but she was still grinning.

"There is nothing stuffy about you, darlin'. And nothing old. Everything's new—especially that laugh. Did you know your eyes sort of dance in that beautiful face when you laugh?"

His eyes had turned dark again, fueled by a fire that was far too warm and far too intimate for her comfort. She felt exposed...and as alive with sensation as if he'd physically touched her.

"You're full of charm, Mr. Thorne. And you do so love to use it, don't you?"

"When it gets results like that, yes, ma'am. I truly do." He reached across the table, took her hand in his. "You have the most kissable mouth. I bet you didn't know that, either, did you?"

Yikes. Okay. Time out. He was way too fast on his

feet for her. And the way she was feeling about him was too confusing.

"If you'll excuse me," she said, pulling her hand from his. "I'll be right back."

Then she hightailed it to the ladies' room while her bones were still in solid form. Another few minutes under his seductive gaze and said bones might just fold like licorice. And then where would she be? Believing he didn't say those things to *all* the girls, that's where. That belief would be a mistake of major proportions.

She knew that for a fact. But knowing it didn't take the sting out of the truth that a teeny, tiny part of her wanted to believe he really thought she was special.

Wasn't that just the most asinine thing? She didn't even like him. Well, she *hadn't* liked him. She still didn't *want* to like him. And yet…she was having fun tonight. Kind of. When the mood struck him, he could be very sweet and attentive and… Stop!

Just stop. This was the same man who had tormented her for the past five years. For all she knew, tonight was just a precursor to another kind of torment. The kind that could leave her wounded instead of just ticked off.

"Had a good time tonight, Chrissie," Jake said as he pulled up in front of her apartment.

As he walked her up the sidewalk to the door of her first-floor apartment, his hands were tucked oh-so casually into his trouser pockets. Of course, to accomplish that he'd had to brush his suit jacket aside. So, of course,

Christine's peripheral vision was filled with the way his white dress shirt hugged an abdomen that, if memory served, exemplified the term *six-pack* abs.

"The dinner was excellent," she said, aware of the warmth of the July night, ultra-aware of the height and the rich scent of the man walking beside her.

"Exceeded only by the company."

When she'd returned to the table after her trip to the ladies' room, she'd very quickly steered him away from the topic of dancing eyes and kissable lips. Fortunately he'd taken her cue and backed off all the Mr. Charm talk. They'd discussed the weather, her work at the hospital and the Royal Museum. When she'd pressed, he'd reluctantly told her about his business—if you counted, "It's doing well," as talking about it.

Since he hadn't seemed to want to talk about it any more than she'd wanted to discuss her family, they'd opted for talk about their alma maters. She was an Aggie and he'd been a Longhorn, and since the two schools were huge interstate rivals, verbal competition about which university was better had kept them occupied through the ride back to her apartment.

But now he was in flirt mode again. And she was going to nip that in the bud because no good could come from her falling for his practiced lines. She had it all planned in her head. She would turn to him when they reached her door, shake his hand, thank him for dinner and get while the getting was good.

She no longer cared that they hadn't sealed the deal

over Jess Golden's things. She'd revisit the issue another time when she wasn't so confused. With all his charming talk and heated looks and walk-on-the-wild-side banter, he'd thrown her totally off-kilter.

She wasn't used to feeling so off balance. She didn't know how to handle the sensation. But she did know how to handle him.

Thank you, handshake, good night. A good, solid plan.

"Thank you," she said when they reached her front door and focused on the hand she extended. "Good night."

Long moments passed and he just stood there.

Finally she was forced to look up and meet his gaze.

Damn him, he was smiling.

Her lungs deflated on a slow, weary sigh. "What's so funny now?"

"You, sweet cheeks. You are a laugh a minute." The warmth and affection in his voice and his expression stirred a herd of butterflies into flight in her tummy. "But then, I'm easily entertained. Come here. Let me show you how easy I am."

And then he kissed her. Just like that. No long, lingering meeting of eyes in the moonlight as a prelude. No dodging and weaving or wondering when it was going to happen.

One minute he was a safe three feet away announcing his intentions. The next he gathered her gently into his arms and lowered his head.

Did she fight it? No.

Did she want to fight it? Um. Guess not.

That was the surprise of the century.

She stood there, her head tipped back, watching as that beautiful mouth descended. Actually she more than watched. She actually rose up on her tiptoes to meet him. Then she lifted her hands to his biceps to steady herself, to mold herself closer. And she let him show her exactly how easy he was.

He showed her just fine. He was easy like a down comforter on a cool winter night. Easy like a daydream on a lazy summer afternoon. The caress of his mouth as he opened it over hers was slow and sweet, soft and undemanding.

It was wonderful. It was amazing. She didn't think about raising her arms to his neck and burying her fingers in the hair at his nape. She simply did it, only tactilely aware of the silky softness of his hair, the warmth and strength of the muscle beneath his skin, the heady heat and hardness of him against her as he wrapped her closer, deeper into his big body.

And he was big. So strong yet so gentle as he cradled her against him, changed the angle of his mouth over hers and with a groan that reverberated against her breasts, took the kiss to a whole other level.

His mouth urged hers open. His tongue entered when she gladly acquiesced. Through the ringing in her ears and the trembling of her entire body, she recognized his hunger, melted into the pleasure, rode the wave of mutual need.

She felt dizzy with the knowledge that a man like him truly could be aroused by a woman like her. He definitely was aroused, no hiding that with her belly pressed against his this way. She felt the power of that knowledge surge through her like a current. Imagined the full measure of his passion with a shiver, then felt wrenched from the heat of sensual pleasure to the cool rush of reality when his big hands rose to hers and untangled them from around his neck and he set her physically away.

"Whoa," he said in a voice that was gruff with passion. With one small step he put a mile of distance between them.

She blinked, her lips pulsing and swollen, her entire body buzzing on sensual overload.

"Whoa," he said again. Then he shook his head and after a look that was searching and stunned and wary, he turned on his heel and hightailed it down the walk to his car.

That was it. Not another word.

A little stunned, Christine watched him go. Got the distinct impression that he was running away, when only moments ago he hadn't been able to get close enough fast enough.

She was still standing in the same spot when he peeled away from the curb. Her lips were still tingling from his kiss when she went to bed half an hour later. And her mind—Lord above, her mind was still spinning.

Her experience with sex was limited and for the most part unsatisfying. Her fault, is what she'd always figured.

She didn't do well with touching. Didn't do well with trust. Sexual encounter made for more tension than passion. But Jacob Thorne had just proven there were exceptions to some rules she'd taken for granted as unbreakable.

To her utter surprise, she'd liked being touched by him. She'd loved being kissed by him. Trust hadn't even been an issue. Or maybe it had been the entire issue and she'd instinctively trusted him when he'd drawn her in, wrapped her tight and made love to her mouth with the enthusiasm and the expertise of a lover. One who sensed exactly what she wanted, exactly what she needed, and made it clear with the touch of his hand, the heat of his mouth, that he knew precisely how to deliver.

And he had delivered—until he'd abruptly dragged himself away, looked at her as though he didn't know how she'd ended up in his arms and hadn't been able to leave fast enough.

He had acted as though it had been a colossal mistake to kiss her.

But it hadn't felt like a mistake. It had felt...wow. It had felt incredible.

Now, however, she felt incredibly confused.

And alone. Most of all, alone.

Of all the things in the world she'd ever wanted, ever dreamed or fantasized about, being alone for the rest of her life hadn't been one of them. Never had she been more aware that the choices she'd made and the barriers she'd erected might have guaranteed that she always would be alone.

She was so lost in those dismal conclusions that it didn't even dawn on her until much later that they had never gotten around to discussing the hoops she had to jump through to get him to give her Jess Golden's things.

Six

Later that night, Jake sat at the bar in the Texas Cattleman's Club nursing a beer. Normally he found a certain amount of contentment in the sprawling, exclusive gentlemen's club Henry "Tex" Langley had established nearly one hundred years ago. Everything about the place was male, from the rich, dark paneling, heavy leather furniture and massive fireplace to the huge oil paintings, animal heads and antique guns displayed on the walls.

He needed the no-frills, no-female atmosphere. But tonight instead of enjoying it, he was brooding. He'd left Chrissie Travers over two hours ago. Kissable, crushable, vulnerable, incredible Chrissie Travers.

Lord above, could he get lost in that woman's kisses. And he had been lost—without-a-map-or-a-compass lost—until his brains had finally come in and, with a mad scramble, he'd gotten his bearings. Then he'd run, not walked, away from the glut of emotions that had scuffled with his better judgment.

He kept seeing her and her sweet, soft, swollen lips. Her and her gray-green eyes, wide open and wondering. *Whoa.*

Seemed to be the word of the night.

"You look like you're in a mood."

He glanced over his shoulder, surprised to see his twin brother, Connor, ease onto a bar stool beside him. It was like looking into a mirror. Folks still remarked that if it weren't for the hair, they wouldn't be able to tell the twins apart. Connor wore his dark brown hair in a clipped military cut—a holdover from his Army Ranger days. Jake preferred to let his hair grow, sometimes to the point of being shaggy—a holdover from his rebellious youth.

"*I'm* in a mood?" Jake grunted and returned his attention to his beer. "This from Mr. Mood Swing himself."

Immediately Jake regretted the offhand remark. Par for the course, he always seemed to say the wrong thing to Connor lately, and in this case Connor was right. Jake *was* in a mood.

Jake motioned to the bartender. "Give us two more, would ya, Joe? Seems the Thorne boys are of the same mind tonight." He turned toward his brother, prepared to make atonement. "What brings you out this time of night?"

It was getting close to last call. Connor wasn't known for frequenting the bar, so Jake had been surprised when his brother had sat beside him. Jake had been so mired in his own pickle, though, he hadn't given it much thought at first.

"Couldn't sleep," Connor said with a throwaway shrug as he reached for his longneck and took a deep pull.

Tell me about it, Jake thought but didn't say as much. Ever since he'd left Chris Travers standing at her front door, he'd been as revved as a DuPont Chevy on NAS-CAR race day.

"Figured there'd be a poker game goin' on," Connor added while Jake huddled over his beer and tried to forget the things that prickly woman had done to him. Like turn him on, fire him up and wring him out.

"Game broke up about midnight," Jake said. He'd turned down the offer to join in. In his state of mind, he would have lost the business and wouldn't even have cared.

But he wasn't so self-consumed that he didn't notice something was up with Connor. Jake cared about his brother. Connor hadn't been the same since returning from the Middle East. He had followed their father's footsteps in an attempt to win the old man's favor by becoming a U.S. Army Airborne Ranger and then an engineer.

Jake, an adrenaline junkie, had opted for a different type of career adventure. After his four-year hitch with the Army, during which time he took college credit classes that he finished up at University of Texas, he'd gone to work for Red Adair fighting oil-well fires.

He'd became so addicted to the danger, he'd wanted a greater hand in it and left Red to form his own company, Hellfire, International. While his twin had been fighting terrorists in the Middle East, Jake made his own statement for freedom and patriotism by fighting oil fires in the same war-torn countries.

They'd both been there. Now they were back. And some things had never changed. Such as sensing when there was a problem.

"Heard from the old man lately?" Jake asked, wondering if a recent set-to with their father was at the root of Connor's dark mood.

Connor's grunt gave Jake his answer. Yeah, Connor had had another tangle with their father. Even though his folks had moved to Florida, James Thorne still could reach out and touch all kinds of raw nerves.

When Connor had retired from active duty, he'd made the ultimate sacrifice. He'd taken over the family engineering firm when their father retired. Jake owed his twin big-time for that. It had gotten the old man off his back.

Some would call his father's repeated wish for Jake to take over the business the burden of the favored son. Jake called it something else—damn unfortunate.

He knew that their father's blatant favoritism toward Jake had always made Connor feel like second banana. Oh, Connor had never said as much. He didn't have to. Actions spoke louder than any words. Even when they were kids, Jake often had talked his way out of a sound pounding with the old man's belt. Connor, on the rare occasion he bucked the old man, never even tried. He just took the beating. And as a result, Jake had watched Connor turn deeper into himself, bottle up his pain and anger until the dark mood would hit him.

Like tonight.

"Tell you what, brother mine," Jake said, slinging an arm over Connor's shoulder, knowing there were some things embedded so deep, no amount of heart-to-heart sessions would drag them out, "how about we blow this place, dive into a case of brew and the two of us get rip-roaring drunk? I haven't tied one on in a coon's age. You game?"

That finally made Connor smile. "Must be woman trouble."

"Got that right," Jake muttered as he dug into his hip pocket for his wallet, then tossed some bills onto the bar. Big-time woman trouble.

What in the hell was he going to do about Chrissie Travers? Things had gotten out of hand tonight. He'd set out to do a little seducing. Just a little good-natured fun and games.

But then he'd kissed her…and she'd come alive like a flame set to a candle.

And it hadn't seemed so much like fun and games after that. He'd felt the subtle give of her body, the gentle swell of her breasts against his chest. It had been much more than a kiss to her. Not to him, of course. No, he thought and wiped at a bead of sweat that had pooled on his forehead. Not to him.

Now he knew what that niggling sense of catastrophe he'd been experiencing on and off all night was about. He'd screwed up. When he'd crossed the line from teasing to appreciating, from tormenting to kissing... Well, he'd changed the dynamics between Chrissie and him.

When she was a prickly little prude, he'd been as safe as a Boy Scout on a supervised campout. But when she'd transformed into a vibrant, alluring woman before his eyes, he'd ditched his Scout troop in favor of a little sweet talk and seduction. And the safety factor had flown out the proverbial window.

Words such as *serious* and *relationship* and *future* and other scary notions leaped to mind. He simply didn't do those things. Not any more. Jake had gone the marriage route once and he'd gotten used, burned, battered and beaten. Ever since, fun and games had been his stock-in-trade. Just fun. Just games.

Prissy Chrissie, however, kissed as though she planned on changing the rules and the stakes. And well, that just wasn't going to happen. Not to him. Not again.

That's why he'd walked. Before the harm. Before the foul.

So why was he sitting here fighting the urge to walk right back to Chrissie? Get a better, longer, bigger taste of what he'd just walked away from?

He dragged a hand over his face. He had to think. He had to think about this a lot. But not tonight.

"Come on," he said. "My place. Gotta be something on ESPN to take our minds off what ails us."

"This time of night? Nothing but reruns," Connor said, walking beside him out of the club.

"Good enough for me," Jake said.

When the light finally dawned, it lit up Christine's world like a ten-thousand-watt bulb and darn near blinded her. That's why Monday at noon she had a mission on her mind when she maneuvered her flashy, brand-new red convertible—purchased just fifteen minutes ago when she traded in her used tan compact—into a space in front of Hellfire, International.

She was turning over new leaves left and right. No more dull and drab and ultrasafe for Christine Travers. From now on it was flash and fire, razzle and dazzle. She was filled with determination to change a few more things when she fed the meter, drew a deep breath and headed into the building.

She'd thought about her meeting-slash-date with Jake Thorne all weekend. Mostly she'd thought about the way he'd kissed her. She'd gotten all warm and tingly inside. And she liked the feeling of excitement and anticipation. She'd considered his offer to teach her about walking on the wild side. And she liked the prospect of treading a new path. Yeah, she was still getting used to this brave new Chris.

She had Jake to thank for this awakening. The man, she thought with a smile as she pressed the elevator button that would take her to Jake's fourth-floor office, was full of the devil and full of life and teasing and fun.

After five years of scowling over his antics, cursing him for his insensitivity, she'd done a one-eighty. She now was convinced that he'd had the right idea after all. She'd been doing it all wrong.

She wasn't sure of the exact moment when she'd come to that conclusion. It wasn't that the bulb had been off one second, then suddenly burned full blast the next. No, the wattage had steadily increased over the weekend. It had finally powered to full glare about the same time she'd started asking herself what her strait-laced, all-work-no-play mind-set had netted her all these years. And she'd realized she didn't like all the answers.

Well, she was going to ask some new questions. Starting today.

"Hi, Janice."

Jake's secretary looked up from her desk when Christine breezed in the door. "Well, hello. You're look-ing...bubbly," the secretary said with a curious smile.

Christine felt bubbly. And it was about time. "Is Jake in?"

Janice picked up the handset. "Let me see if he's busy."

Christine hadn't even settled into a chair when Janice said, "You can go in. Great outfit, by the way," she added with an approving nod. "I love what you've done with your hair."

Christine's new plan had called for new look. That's why she'd headed out to the mall Sunday afternoon and spent some of her moldy money—Alison's words—on some snappy new sandals, a pair of snug white capri pants and a white spaghetti-strap tank. Over top she wore an off-the-shoulder, light-as-air silk-scarf blouse in a soft pink print that gave the entire outfit a breezy, sexy and fun look. She'd also gotten a makeover. A short, sassy haircut and some makeup secrets made her look vibrant instead of invisible.

The look fit her mood. Right up until the moment she walked into Jake's office. Then all of her hard-won confidence crumpled in the face of what she planned to do.

Can I really do this?

Jake had a smile firmly in place. The smile, however, deflated like a leaky balloon as he looked her up and down.

"Chrissie. This is a…surprise."

More than a surprise. Christine could see that by the way his dark eyebrows were pulled together. He seemed wary about what her presence in his office meant. Was he worried about her reaction, given that he'd kissed her silly Saturday night, then galloped out of Dodge as fast as three hundred and fifty horses could take him? Maybe more than wary. Maybe he was worried sick that she'd read too much into that kiss.

Well, she hadn't. But she did intend to stay the course.

"Sorry to barge in like this. I was wondering if you had a minute to talk."

He leaned back in his chair. Tossed down his pen and gave her another appraising look. "Well, um, sure.

What's on your mind? Wait. Stupid question. You're here about Jess Golden's things."

"Not exactly."

Okay. This was much harder than she'd thought it would be. She took a deep breath, let it out and put it all on the line.

She blurted out what she wanted from him.

Then she waited for the fallout as a stunned and, if she wasn't mistaken, panicked look froze on Jake's handsome face.

"You want me to what?"

Oh, God, Jake thought. This was not what he needed today.

"I want you to make good on your offer. I want lessons on how to walk on the wild side."

No. No. No. He'd had it all worked out. It was a done deal. He'd crossed the wrong line with Chrissie Saturday night—a line he'd decided he wasn't going to cross again, no way, no how, no time. He was going to forget about her innocent, lusty kisses and go back to being her biggest pain in the butt.

That was the safe way.

But now here she was, all girly and gorgeous and pink and sexy as hell with that handkerchief of a top sliding off her left shoulder and leaving it bare. She'd done something to her hair, too. Cut it in a sassy do that gave the illusion she had just gotten out of bed and run her fingers through it—or a lover had.

And her lips. Lord, they looked plump and pouty, painted the prettiest shade that had him licking his own lips over the thought of licking the color off hers.

Double hell. Just when he'd had all his ducks lined up in a neat and tidy row, Miss Quick-Change Artist had come rushing in and sent them scattering in every which direction.

"Um…Jake?"

Her voice was thick with uncertainty, and suddenly he felt guilty. It wasn't her fault that he wanted to turn back the clock to a time when the hot-looking woman standing anxiously in his doorway had been a stodgy, prickly, schoolmarm-of-yore type who had interested him only from the standpoint of how much of a rise he could tease out of her.

Funny how the tables had turned on *that* level. If he wasn't careful, the memory of that amazing kiss they'd shared coupled with the way she looked today might make him rise to the occasion. Literally.

He manufactured a stiff smile when she eased his office door shut behind her.

"Chrissie. I was joking when I said that."

You could dress the girl up in soft, sexy clothes, but you couldn't quite iron the starch out of the girl. Her chin went up and her shoulders stiffened, and suddenly he understood how much this request had cost her. "So you didn't mean it when you said you wanted to volunteer to teach me how to loosen up?"

"Um, well," was the best response he could manage

to say because he couldn't stop looking at her, knowing that this new Chrissie presented a whole lot more complications than the old one. The one who would have poked him to death with her quills instead of melting into his arms like a candy kiss.

"Life's short, Jake. You above all men should know that."

"Well, yeah, but—"

"And you got me thinking Saturday night. Well, not just Saturday night but all weekend. Do you know how old I am?" she asked, abruptly shifting gears.

She didn't wait for him to answer but barged on like a steamroller on a diesel high. It was as if she had to get the words out all at once or she'd lose her nerve.

"Twenty-eight. I'm twenty-eight years old and I still don't know what I want to be when I grow up. I don't truly know what I want out of life and you want to know why?"

"Um—"

"I'll tell you why."

He puffed out a breath between his cheeks and prepared to listen.

"Because I've never given myself an opportunity to think about what I really wanted. How sad is that?"

He opened his mouth but no sound came out because she continued to speak, her tone growing reflective and regretful.

"I've been too busy toeing the line. And what has it gotten me?"

He didn't bother to try to respond. Clearly she'd

come here on a mission to get some things off her chest—her soft, voluptuous chest that at the moment was pressed quite nicely against her silky blouse as she drew in a shaky breath.

"What it's gotten me is respectability. Okay, fine. Respectability is good. And it's gotten me security. Also good. But has it gotten me contentment?"

"I'm thinking the answer might be no?" he said cautiously when she paused and appealed to him as if she really did expect an answer.

"No is exactly right. I do not have contentment. Not for even a second have I led what I consider to be a contented life. Dull, yes. Contented, no. There has to be at least a little excitement for a person to be content, right? Well, where's my excitement? Where are my thrills? Where are my…my magic moments?"

Oh, sweetie, don't cry, he thought when her lower lip started quivering in the face of a self-assessment that was both harsh and humiliating. On top of everything else, he didn't think he could take it if she cried.

He stood and made his way around his desk. Easing a hip on the corner, he crossed his arms over his chest to keep from holding her close and telling her there was still hope.

But then a big, glistening teardrop spilled down her cheek and he was a goner.

He reached for her and patted her back clumsily. "It's not really so bad," he lied kindly.

"It's…awful. P-Prissy Chrissie," she sputtered

against his chest. "That's what they call me behind my back. Did you know that?"

Oh, yeah. He knew. Was probably the worst offender. Her little sniffle twisted the knife of guilt deeply embedded in his gut. He patted with a little more sympathy.

"The worst part is, they're right. Well, they *were* right. I've been nothing but a…a goal-oriented workaholic. All my life I've been so focused on my need for respectability and stability and safety that I've ignored my other needs. A woman's needs," she said and lifted her head to look up into his eyes.

Gulp. Not those big hazel eyes. He was a sucker for her eyes.

"I want to know what it feels like to be appreciated as a woman. To be desired by a man. To have power over a man."

Sweetheart, if you only knew how much power you had right now. She could have brought him to his knees. First with guilt. Then with the desire to kiss her tears away, to bite gently into the quivering softness of her lush lower lip.

He resisted. Only God knew how, because she felt so soft and warm and wonderful cuddled up against him. But he'd made up his mind Saturday night between a six-pack and an ESPN classic football game. He was nipping in the bud this new twist to their relationship that he'd had the misfortune to initiate.

Chris Travers needed a man who would stick around. One who was in for the long haul. Didn't matter how much Jake loved her kisses, didn't matter that he found her a sweet surprise, a sexy temptation, he was not the kind of man she needed.

"I'm a spinster," she said on another teary sigh. "An old maid. And all because I've been too scared to take a chance on life."

"Aw, Chrissie," he said, feeling sad that she was bullying herself this way.

"But that's all going to change," she said, finding her composure again and pushing away from him.

Just look at those freckles, he thought. Dusting the bridge of her nose, riding on her cheeks like little angel kisses. It made him feel soft and sentimental in his chest. And hard in other places.

Until she said, "And you're the man who's going to make it happen."

Seven

Jake's mouth opened as wide as his eyes. "What? *Me?* What am I going to make happen?"

"For five years you've needled me, teased me, made fun of me and in general goaded me into burying my feet deeper into my principles and my head deeper into the sand. Well, Saturday night changed all that. You were nice to me. In fact, you were into me. I liked it."

Damn. "Chris—"

"Oh, don't worry," she said, some of the old starchy Chrissie back in her speech and her bearing. "I know you were just playing. I know what you are. You're a flirt and a good-time guy. And you were just being you on Saturday night because I wasn't being me. At least,

I wasn't being the old me. I was being the new me when I didn't even realize I wanted me to be a different me."

His head was starting to hurt. "Huh?"

She waved a hand. "Doesn't matter. What does matter is that you offered to teach me how to loosen up and have fun and I'm going to hold you to it. Starting right now."

And the next thing he knew, she kissed him. She reached up, placed her hands on either side of his face and pulled his mouth down to hers. There wasn't any finesse to it. It was all about impulse and determination and flat-out moxie.

It should have been funny. But for some reason he thought it was sweet. At least, he did during the moments he wasn't alternating between panic that warned him he could easily go down for the count here and a flat out case of pure, animal lust.

That mouth. She did have a way with her mouth. It wasn't practiced. It wasn't expert. But, oh, was it enthusiastic. And that enthusiasm was infectious. He hadn't planned to kiss her back. But there was the surprise factor. And the heat factor. And the warm, soft woman factor that, combined, sucked him in, egged him on and dragged him under.

He widened his legs, pulled her between them and dived into the kiss like a pearl diver on a treasure hunt. He urged her mouth open, swept inside her sweet, wet heat with his tongue while pressing her into his growing erection with one hand at the small of her back. His other hand pressed between her shoulder blades, encouraging the pressure of her breasts against his chest.

And sweet ambrosia, she tasted good. The soft sounds she made deep in her throat fostered a low growl of his own that had him leaning back on the top of his desk, bringing her with him. He heard something crash to the floor, didn't care what it was because her full weight covered him now—sexy and hot and pressing in all the right places.

If their sudden horizontal tango gave her pause, she didn't let on. In fact, she really got into the kiss then. She'd let go of his face and buried her hands in his hair, all the while squirming and sighing and doing a little pressing of her own.

He loved it. Loved the honest lust. The exuberant response. But most of all he loved the way they fit, the heady friction as she moved above him, dragging him deeper into the heat of the moment and further away from the consequences.

He was ready to take it to the next level. Make love to her right there on the top of his desk, in the middle of Monday, when she lifted her head. Looked down into his eyes through those drowsy hazel eyes of hers and in the most slumberous, seductive voice he'd ever heard, she whispered, "Consider that payment for lesson one. Come through with lesson two and there'll be more where that came from."

Then, as if she hadn't just played the most amazing game of tonsil tag he'd ever been a party to, she pushed herself off him, straightened her top and left him flat on his back.

"When you do come up with lesson number two," she said, turning around with one hand on the door handle, "give me a call." Then she left him. Hot and bothered. Hard and hungry.

When the blood returned to his head several long minutes later, he eased himself to a sitting position. When he could take a breath that didn't smell of her—something fresh and citrusy—he carefully stood.

For the longest time he just stared at the closed door. Finally he raked both hands through his hair, swore, then dropped into his desk chair. He let his head fall back and stared at the ceiling.

What the hell had just happened here?

He felt as if he'd been hit by a tank. At the very least, by a whirlwind in the guise of Chrissie Travers.

Prissy? He'd never again think of her that way.

But he would think of her. She'd made sure of that.

He'd be thinking about just how silky her skin might be. How those soft breasts would feel pressed against his palm, how they'd taste on his tongue. About how much heat the two of them could generate on a big bed instead of a hard desk.

None of that was supposed to happen. He wasn't supposed to kiss her again, to flirt with her again, to charm her again, let alone think about making love to her.

But she's the one who had done the kissing. And the flirting. And the charming.

And the challenging, he realized as a tight knot of grudging respect twisted into anger. The minx had turned the tables on him. She'd leveled a dare. He was the one who had always been in control of their relationship—if you could call what they'd had until Saturday night a relationship. Mostly it had been a good-natured—at least on his part—razzfest. He teased. She bristled. He'd liked it that way.

But then he'd been stupid enough to kiss her. He'd used the weekend to put that kiss into perspective, chalked it up to stupidity. End of story. Until the woman had barged in here, added another chapter to the book and confused the hell out of him with her talk about "old me" and "new me" before attacking him with those sizzling, mind-bending kisses.

Now he was in a daze. And that just plain fried his circuits. He did not get bent out of shape over a woman. It wasn't allowed. It wasn't supposed to happen.

So why had it?

He stood and walked to the window. Maybe he was bored. Since he'd damaged his lungs in that damn fire five years ago, he'd had to be satisfied with the management end of his own business. Sure, it was rewarding. But it was dull. He'd joined the Texas Cattleman's Club hoping for a little excitement, but so far all the thrill he'd gotten was to listen to the exploits of other club members. Hearing those stories about saving countries or princesses only served to remind Jake of his limitations.

Chrissie had been a handy distraction. One that he'd let get out of hand.

Well, there was only one thing to do about it, he decided as the haze began to lift. This couldn't go on. He had to regain the upper hand. And he knew how to do it.

He was going to call her bluff.

Little Chrissie wanted to take a walk on the wild side? Well, then, he would give her the walk of her life. That would put an end to her hit-and-run kisses. Put an end to her messing with his head.

He'd come up with something so wild and so foreign to her straitlaced nature that she'd run like a rabbit and he'd never see her sweet face again. Yeah. He'd fix her little red wagon and reclaim his equilibrium in the process.

He felt marginally better about the situation until he dragged a hand over his face and realized how unsteady he still was.

Why in the hell hadn't he let her win the bid on Jess Golden's things? Then none of this would be happening.

She'd done it.

Between sharp bouts of disbelief that left her tummy tumbling and moments of pride at her own audacity, Christine couldn't stop grinning. She'd marched into Jake Thorne's domain and told him what she thought, told him what she expected from him. Then she'd kissed him.

Well, okay, there had been a little waffling in there, but she'd gotten it together. Oh, had she gotten it together.

Another one of those waves of disbelief swamped her as she signaled for a left turn and headed out of the city. She'd shocked him. Heck, she'd shocked herself. Never in her life had she initiated a kiss. Never in her life had she experienced such a strong sexual reaction. Okay, so her experience was severely limited, but could it get any hotter than that kiss in Jake's office? On his desk?

She wasn't sure where her actions had come from—instinct maybe. Maybe from years of watching movies and reading books and living vicariously through them. Whatever, she'd been a tiger.

She felt good. She felt great! The sun was high and hot, her brand-new convertible's top was down and the wind whipped her hairstyle around her face—something she'd never allowed with her longer hair. It was freeing. And exciting.

"It's the new me!" she shouted into the wind, inched her speed up to a shocking two miles per hour above the speed limit and switched her radio station from the classics to classic rock. She felt like a little kid writing on the walls with crayons or a teenager skipping class.

Actually she was skipping work. Technically she was taking a personal day—something she never did just for the heck of it. It felt naughty. And, wonder of wonders, she liked it.

She couldn't wait to call Alison to tell her what was going on.

And she couldn't wait to hear from Jake to find out what the second lesson would be.

There would be another lesson. She may have discovered some new sides to Jake Thorne during the past few days, but there was one thing about the man she'd always known.

He never backed down from a dare. He wouldn't back down from this one.

"Bring it on," she said aloud. Whatever he fired at her, she was up to it. "The new me is up to it."

The new her wasn't deluding herself into believing that what was going on between her and Jake was a long-term notion. She wasn't foolish enough to think that she was the one who could tame him for a serious relationship when any number of beautiful, sexy women hadn't been able to accomplish the same.

No, she wasn't that foolish. She simply was ready to experience life. For some reason, she trusted Jake to be the man to help her. And when the challenge was over and she'd had her fill, she'd be ready to walk away.

It helped to know what Jake Thorne was—a game player. He couldn't help it. And she wouldn't change him. Even if she wanted to.

The thought of things between them ending—before they'd even really begun—flooded her with an unexpected sadness. She turned up the radio and, at the top of her lungs, sang along with the Boss about being born to run.

Jake left the office early that day and hightailed it to the Cattleman's Club for a little diversion. He breathed a sigh of relief when one of his buddies, Logan Voss, spotted him and motioned him over to join a poker game. A friendly game of five-card stud was exactly what Jake needed to take his mind off Chrissie and the way she'd turned him inside out yet again.

"So, how's it shakin', Jake?" Logan asked as Jake hung his black Stetson on a brass hat rack in the corner of the bar.

"Can't complain. How about you boys?"

He got what he'd expected—mumbled "fines" and head nods. While members of the club often tackled matters of grave importance and danger within these walls, it was also a haven. As a rule, a man didn't come to the Cattleman's Club to talk about his troubles. He came here to get away from them, to simply hang out with men of like minds.

Of all of his friends at the club, he felt a particular kinship to Logan Voss. Voss ran a large cattle ranch just outside of town. Like Jake, the rugged rancher, who was a hands-on owner, was divorced. Unlike Jake who took pains to see that no one saw his pain, Logan's scars occasionally showed in the bleak look in his eyes and the weary set of his shoulders. Or maybe Jake was just sensitive to Logan's situation since he'd gone through an ugly divorce himself.

"You in, Thorne?" Mark Hartman asked. "Or you gonna sit there and admire your cards the rest of the night?"

"Yeah, yeah, I'm in," Jake said and called Hartman's good-natured haranguing.

Jake didn't know Mark Hartman as well as he knew Logan, but he liked what the guy stood for. Jake didn't know the entire story, but the retired soldier had lost his wife in a violent mugging. Mark played his cards—and his feelings—pretty close to the vest, too. The African-American appeared to be independently wealthy but still spent hours at his gym where he gave self-defense classes to women. No one had to wonder what motivated him.

"Read 'em and weep, boys." This came from the fourth man at the table, Gavin O'Neal, as he laid down a diamond flush.

Jake groaned and tossed in his cards. He hated this run of luck. But how loudly could one complain about losing to the sheriff? A decent one at that. O'Neal had been a wild man in his day, but he took the shiny badge that he wore on his chest seriously. The badge also didn't hurt his standing with women. As a rule, Jake loved to give O'Neal grief about his reputation.

Tonight, though, Jake just wasn't in much of a joking mood—mainly because of one particular woman giving him so much grief.

O'Neal dealt Jake another stellar hand. Not. He arranged his cards, rolled his eyes and folded. When Voss won the hand, Jake was down fifty bucks—and he hadn't been in the game a full hour. He was starting to think his luck had deserted him altogether when Voss dealt him a pair of queens. Finally. A bidding hand. He was about to raise Gavin's bet when a commotion by the front door had the entire table on their feet.

"What the hell?"

It was Nita Windcroft. Her violet eyes were shooting sparks and the slim young woman, who had recently taken on one helluva responsibility when she'd assumed management of her father's horse farm, appeared to be in one high and mighty snit.

"Sheriff," she said, marching toward the table. "You've got to do something."

O'Neal met her halfway across the bar and laid a settling hand on her arm. "Good Lord, Nita, settle down before you bust a vein. Not another word until you calm down. Take a deep breath now. That's it. Give me another one. Okay. Now tell me what's wrong." He steered her toward the table where the men had been playing.

Even off duty and out of uniform, Gavin had an air of command that Nita responded to.

"The Devlins are at it again," she said, rage coloring her voice. "And if you don't put a stop to it, so help me, I will. I can't let them destroy my ranch."

"Okay, Nita. Settle down," Gavin repeated with a soothing calm that seemed to make Nita at least stop and take stock of her surroundings.

Besides their table, only a half a dozen other TCC members sat in the bar. After Nita's initial outburst, they all returned to their respective conversations.

"You want to talk to me in private?" Gavin asked.

"I don't care if the whole county hears what those snakes have been up to! You've got to do something."

The Windcrofts and the Devlins had nursed a Hatfield-and-McCoy-style feud for close to a century. Old Jonathan Devlin had liked to keep the situation stirred up, but Jake had thought things would settle down now that Jonathan was gone.

Judging from the look on Nita's face, he'd thought wrong.

If he had his facts straight, the Windcroft-Devlin feud had started when Richard Windcroft lost over half of his land to Nicholas Devlin in a poker game. The Windcrofts always had maintained the game was rigged. A Devlin ended up getting shot and killed over it, and of course, the Windcrofts got the blame. The accusations and squabbles had been going on ever since.

"Why don't you tell me what's going on out at the ranch that's got you so upset, Nita," Gavin suggested.

"In the past few weeks I've been dealing with downed rails, cut fence lines and spooked horses. At first I tried to write it off as wear and tear, but then I found wire cutters by a downed section and some of my new board fences have been broken, as well. I spent three days rounding up stock from the last time those bastards did their dirty work. But the last straw, the very last straw—they poisoned my horse feed."

Nita's cheeks were fiery red. "If my foreman hadn't noticed something off, there's no telling how much stock I would have lost. It's bad enough I'm treating over a dozen head of very sick horses—some of them my customers'—but it will cost me a small fortune to replace that tainted feed. And do you have any idea what this is going to do to my business once word gets out? It could ruin me. Not to mention, I'm worried sick about the horses. Only a Devlin would stoop so low as to try to kill innocent animals."

No wonder Nita was upset, Jake thought. The Windcroft ranch boarded and trained horses. She'd start to lose customers if they felt the safety of their stock was compromised. She was leveling some pretty serious charges, and the Devlins were prominent citizens in Royal. Tom Devlin was even a member of the Cattleman's Club and Jake considered him a friend.

"Those are pretty strong allegations, Nita," Gavin warned, echoing Jake's thoughts. "You have some proof that the Devlins are behind this?"

"Who else would it be? They've finally come up with a way to ruin us. It's what they've always wanted. And they'll shut us down if they aren't stopped!"

"Have you had any direct threats on your life?" Gavin asked.

"My life is my ranch, so you can play it anyway you like.

"Okay, no," she admitted when Gavin gave her a stern look. "I haven't been personally threatened, but that doesn't mean it won't come to that. I'm worried about my stock. I'm worried about my help. Now, what are you going to do about it?"

"Come on," Gavin said. "Let's go down to the station. You can write out a statement and I'll dispatch an officer to your ranch to take stock of all that's happened. Maybe he can find a lead on who's doing this."

"I told you who's doing it. And I want to press charges," Nita insisted.

"Do you have anything—anything but your gut instinct—tying the Devlins to this?"

Nita's silence was Gavin's answer.

"Go ahead," he said. "I'll meet you at the station."

"I know what that means," she said, her tone expressing her anger. "It means you can't do anything. Okay fine. You can't. You have to follow the letter of the law. But what about you?" she asked, turning to Jake, Mark and Logan. "I know it's supposed to be a secret but it's common knowledge that you TCC guys get involved in situations like this when people are in danger."

Whoa, Jake thought. The club's missions were kept under wraps, so it was a little unsettling to hear Nita announce that their covert operations weren't all that covert. But more unsettling was the fact that Nita felt she was in danger at the hands of a fellow club member and wanted them to investigate. Even though from the sound of things there was really nothing definitive to indicate either danger or Tom Devlin's involvement.

"Nita," Jake said, "I feel real bad for what's happening out there, sweetie. Hell, I'm sure we all do. But for all we know, you're just the unfortunate and random victim of some ugly pranks. Anyone could be responsible. Kids. Vagrants. As to the feed, have you had it tested? Is it possible you just got a bad batch from the elevator?"

"No, I haven't had it tested. It just happened today and I've been too busy saving horses to investigate."

"So, when did you get your last batch of feed?" he pressed.

"Yesterday," she said defensively, "but we always order the same mix from the same elevator, so it's not likely that they're responsible."

Jake cut a glance at the others. Mark, Logan and Gavin all wore looks that said exactly what Jake was thinking. Most likely she'd just gotten a bad batch of feed, but in her panic over the possibility of losing the horses, she'd decided someone needed to take the rap and the Devlins were the most likely target.

"Check with the elevator," Jake said gently. "If you come up blank there after the feed is tested, then maybe we'll consider looking into it."

"Consider?" Her eyes snapped with fire. "Thanks. Thanks so much for nothing."

She stomped out of the club in as much of a huff as when she'd stomped in.

"That's one upset woman," Logan remarked.

"Can't blame her," Jake said. "She's stubborn and outspoken and I've known her to go to great lengths to get her way, but I've never known her to lie about anything. This is her livelihood that's being threatened. I'm sure she's scared."

"Let's keep our ears open for word from the elevator regarding the feed," Mark suggested.

"What about the fences?" Logan asked.

Jake shrugged. "Who knows? Could be kids. Could be any number of possibilities. What do you guys think of checking with Tom Devlin to see if he has any ideas on what's going on?"

"He's out of town right now. Business trip," Gavin said.

"When he comes back, then," Jake said. "We'll find out what he thinks. Man, when old Jonathan was alive, he loved to stir the fire on the Windcroft-Devlin feud every chance he got. I thought maybe after he died that this stupid feud business would die a quiet death, too."

"I should be so lucky," Gavin said on a weary breath. "See you boys. I'd better get down to the station before Nita raises hell with my officers."

"But I was about to get into you for some serious coin," Jake complained, thinking about his pair of queens.

"You can break my bank another night, buddy. I've got a mad woman waiting and it's not going to do any of us any good if I keep her that way too long."

Didn't it just figure? Jake thought. These days there always seemed to be a woman complicating things for him. Nita was leaning on the club members for help, and his pair of queens hadn't shown up until after he'd dropped a bundle and the game was over. Then there was Chrissie. Lord. She had materialized this afternoon as a different woman, then issued a challenge he couldn't see his way clear to walk away from.

Eight

"**M**y place. Tonight. Midnight. Wear jeans and boots."

Christine's heart knocked her a couple of good ones in her chest when she listened to the message on her answering machine.

That the message was from Jake was without question. She'd recognize his barbed-wire-and-velvet voice anywhere. That he'd answered her challenge so soon—the day after she'd lain her metaphorical cards on the table—was a big surprise.

"So, what are you going to do?"

Christine looked at Alison, who had dropped by after work to check out Chris's sports car.

"I'm going to go. It's what I want."

Alison eyed her with appreciation. "You are serious about this personal alteration, aren't you?"

"Like I said—" Christine made a concentrated attempt not to chew nervously on her lower lip "—I'm tired of playing it safe and dull. I know it sounds funny given our history, but I trust Jake not to hurt me."

"Jake is it? He's not the evil twin or the insensitive jerk anymore? My, my. That must have been some dinner date Saturday night."

"Let's just say the evening opened me up to new possibilities."

"Well, I say, you go, girl. Just…well, be a *little* careful, okay? I don't want to see you get hurt."

"I'll be fine," Christine assured Alison even though she wasn't one hundred percent sure herself. "I know what I'm doing."

Six hours later, however, as Christine pulled into the drive of Jake Thorne's ranch south of Royal, one burning question kept surfacing like a stubborn cork in a choppy sea: *What am I doing?*

She eased her convertible around the circular drive, then stopped in front of a portico that flanked a pair of massive double doors framed in a stucco structure the color of sand.

Money. The place reeked of it with its understated elegance and style. The house was new—one of many in this area where land was sold in five-hundred-acre parcels of rolling hills and the occasional thicket of timber.

Only the wealthy and privileged could afford the property here.

Lot of house for one man, she thought as her gaze roamed over the impressive facade. A light mounted under the portico came on and the front door swung open.

Make that, a lot of man for one woman.

Neither the businessman nor the tease strode out to meet her. A cowboy did. And Jake Thorne as an icon of the American west personified the cowboy mystic in resounding three-dimensional color.

His boots were a rusty-brown color. His Wranglers looked soft and worn and tight. On his head was a black, well-shaped Stetson—black for bad guy, she thought—and his shirt was as white as snow with mother-of-pearl snaps running down his torso and on the breast pockets. The blue bandanna he'd tied around his neck lay in stark contrast against his white shirt and tanned throat. Spurs jingled with every long, purposeful stride.

The only thing missing was a pair of six-shooters strapped on his lean hips. Still, she got the feeling that he was gunning for her.

"Nice wheels," he said by way of greeting as he looked her car over.

"It's new," she said inanely.

One corner of his mouth turned up. Not a smile. Not a sneer. Small clue as to what he was thinking.

"Got your boots on?"

She got out of the car and showed him. And his not-a-smile-not-a-sneer expression turned into a frown. Big clue as to what he was thinking.

"Let met guess—those would be new, too?"

She glanced away from his look of disgust at her pretty red boots. "What's wrong with them?"

"I was thinking *cowboy* boots."

"These *are* cowboy boots."

"If you're strutting down Rodeo Drive in California maybe. Not if you're planning to ride a horse."

She'd suspected he had a midnight ride in mind, even though she'd held out hope for something else. She didn't ride. In fact, she'd never ridden—guess the choice of boots might have given that away. Somehow she figured he already knew that, too, but she wasn't going to give him the satisfaction of admitting it.

"These boots will do just fine," she said.

He grunted and shook his head. "Come on." Then he walked away from the house toward a mammoth, pristine white barn.

"This is Cletus," he said opening a box stall.

Inside was what Christine considered to be a very big—strike that, an exceptionally huge—brown horse.

"Does he bite?" She could have kicked herself, but the question was out before she could stop it. Talk about sounding green.

"Only blondes," Jake said, leveling her a look. "But since you'll be on his back, you should be safe."

Her stomach sank toward her knees as she looked up the broad length of him. But she smiled. "Oh. Well. Good."

Jake studied her face. "You have ridden, right?"

"Sure. Lots of times." Why was she playing this game? What did she think it was going to net her?

A broken neck, probably, but something about his smug attitude just wouldn't allow her to let him see that she was scared senseless.

"You two get to know each other," Jake said. "I'll go get my mount."

"Good. Great. I'll be fine," she said, lying through her teeth. "Nice…horse," she whispered when Jake was out of her line of sight. "Be nice, okay? I brought you something."

Again, because she'd figured a ride might be what Jake had in mind, she'd hedged her bets. She fished into her hip pocket and pulled out a sugar lump. She'd heard that horses like sugar.

She'd heard right. Cletus went for the sugar like a bear after honey. It was icky feeding it to him. He snuffled all over her palm before finally lipping the sweet treat into his mouth. When he was finished, he lowered his head and nudged her hip pocket where she'd tucked the rest of the sugar, evidently smelling it there.

"Okay, okay," she said, laughing in spite of herself, and gave him another hit. "Now we're friends, right?"

In answer, the horse nipped at her pocket.

"Hey," she sputtered, stepping back. "Easy on the jeans."

"They as new as your boots?" Jake asked, startling

her as he walked down the aisle of the barn, a big buckskin in tow.

She manufactured a smile. "You're right about the biting thing."

His blue eyes pinned hers in the dimly lit barn. "Any guy is liable to bite if a woman has something in her pants that he wants."

Oh. My. This must be where the walk on the wild side came in. He was letting her know. *You came out here to learn, and I'm just the man to teach you.*

"Busted," she said, conceding that he'd caught her with the sugar but not going anywhere near the sexual innuendo. "Who knew he'd be such a glutton?"

"Offer me sugar. See what kind of a glutton I become."

He gave her another one of those long, smoldering looks that held undertones of all kinds of gluttony, along with shades of warning. She actually thought about turning tail and running as fast and as far as her new red boots would take her.

The old Christine would have run. The new one followed him as he led the two horses out of the barn and into the moonlight.

"Come on. I'll help you up into the saddle," Jake offered. "Cletus is long on leg, and you're just a little short on one end. Um, you always mount from the left, Chrissie."

Face flaming red, Christine walked back around to the horse's left side. "I knew that. I was just checking out the, um, stirrup."

"Sure you were," he said. "Now grab the saddle horn. It's that tall thing right behind the mane and in front of the seat," he added with another shake of his head.

"Well, if I could reach it, it would help," she sputtered, angry with herself for not being better informed and angry with him for knowing it. "Oh, whoa." The next thing she knew, she was airborne.

Jake's strong hands had gripped her around the waist, lifted her up and deposited her on the saddle like a sack of potatoes.

"Here are your reins," he said when she'd managed to push herself to a sitting position. Problem was, she was gripping the saddle horn for dear life and didn't have any intention of letting go, even if it was to take the reins.

"What's he doing?" she asked, near panic when the big body between her legs seemed to pitch and roll like a ship in a rough sea.

"Shifting his weight from one back leg to the other," Jake said, grinning openly now. "You ready to give up the pretense?"

"Yes," she all but whined. "Am I going to get hurt?"

He chuckled. "Not on Cletus. He's a pussycat. And you nailed his soft spot with the sugar, so he's not going to take a chance of dumping you because you have his sugar stash. Just sit easy, rock with the motion and trust him to take you where we want to go."

Trust. There was that word again. And that was what this was all about.

"Well, then, yee haw," she said and smiled when it made him chuckle.

Jake mounted up and they were on the move. The night was warm. The wind that usually kicked up during the day in this part of Texas had mellowed to a breeze. It played gently with her hair, cooling her skin yet somehow warming the night.

Or maybe it was the fear of falling off the horse that made her so warm. More likely it was the prospect of what the evil twin had in mind. Cletus proved to be a real gentleman as he plodded along beneath the stars. So far Jake had been a gentleman, too. Despite the temperature of the night, despite the blanket of stars shining down, she shivered in anticipation of what he had in mind for lesson number two. In all likelihood, being a gentleman was the furthest thing from his mind.

"Greenhorns," Jake sputtered good-naturedly an hour later when he helped Christine down out of the saddle. "How can you live in Texas and be such a greenhorn?"

"Not all of Texas is yippee-yi-yo-ki-yay land, you know," she grumbled. "I grew up in Houston. We had cars."

Cute. She was too cute. And a little sore, if Jake didn't miss his guess. But she was game, he'd give her that. Once she'd found her seat, she'd taken to the midnight ride like a trooper.

Of course, he never would have paired her with a

horse that would have placed her in any danger. Old Cletus was pushing twenty-five, and if a random thought of bucking ever did cross the old boy's mind, Jake was confident it would get lost somewhere between Cletus's head and the execution. So, no, Christine had never been in any danger.

At least, not from the horse.

Not for the first time he told himself that what he had planned was not a good idea. But it would work, if it didn't backfire on him.

"So, is this like a rest stop?" she asked, tugging down on the thighs of her jeans as if they'd crept up and into places they didn't belong.

Places he'd noticed. Places he'd been thinking about way too much as he'd ridden in relative silence beside her, a silence broken only by his limited advice on the finer points of riding and his reassurances that no, Cletus had no intentions of bucking.

He'd noticed other things, as well. Like the way the starlight shined on her silver-gold hair. Like how cute she looked in those ridiculous boots and how tiny her waist was with her white tank top tucked into her jeans.

Who knew that Miss Chrissie was the complete package? Who could have possibly known? If he hadn't seen her dressed to kill Saturday night, if he hadn't felt all those sexy curves against him when they'd kissed—twice now—he never would have guessed it. She'd seemed to make it a mission to disguise that she was even remotely feminine—even though he'd seen glimpses of the china doll lurking beneath all that starch.

Hell, it had crossed his mind a time or two that, as prickly as she was toward him, maybe she played for the other team. He'd never seen her with a guy, never heard of her dating. In fact, when he did see her, she was either alone or with a friend. So, yeah, it had crossed his mind that maybe it wasn't just him that turned her off but that women turned her on. Not that there was anything wrong with that. But, man, what a waste, he thought, watching her now as she stretched her arms above her head and worked out some of the kinks.

Now he knew for sure that she definitely liked the opposite sex. No woman could kiss him the way she had and not be totally into it. It shouldn't have made him so happy because tonight, after all, wasn't about seducing her. Tonight was about scaring her back to where she didn't want to come within ten feet of him except to hurl insults.

Yeah. Tonight was about reestablishing distance, because distance was the best thing he could give her.

"Come on," he said, leading his gelding by the reins. "Let's walk over this rise."

"Oh," she said when she saw what was on the other side of the small hill. "It's beautiful."

The little man-made lake was, for a fact, pretty in the moonlight. But Jake had confidence that what he was about to suggest was going to put the prissy back in

Chrissie and that there wasn't enough "pretty" in the world to entice her to do it.

And then life, as he knew it where she was concerned, could get back to normal.

"So, Chrissie," he said oh-so casually, "let's lose the duds. We're going skinny-dipping."

He could have sworn he heard a teeny, tiny "Help" from her as he hung his hat on a low-hanging branch of a nearby tree.

And when he reached for his belt buckle, he knew he heard one.

Her eyes were as big as dinner plates when he turned toward her.

"Skinny-dipping?"

"As you ordered," he said, undoing the buckle and the metal button on his waistband. "Lesson number two."

He almost felt sorry for her—almost—as he slid down his zipper then tugged his shirttails free. "Any walk on the wild side has to include a midnight dip."

"N-n-nude?" she squeaked out as he shucked his shirt and tossed it to the ground.

"Naturally," he said, sitting on the ground to tug off his boots and socks. When he stood again, he was wearing nothing but his jeans and a smile. "You're falling behind, sweet cheeks," he said and dropped the jeans.

Her little gasp was punctuated by a small, lingering "Oh" that escaped like a sigh.

He gave her a good eyeful, liking a little too much the way her nervous gaze flitted from his face to his chest to his face again, then to his groin—which was liking the way she looked at him a little too much, too. Mixed in with the fear and surprise in her expression was a very female appreciation.

"Time's a-wastin'," he said and showed her his back—just a little too late to hide what her hot looks had done to him. He walked to the bank, waded to midthigh before executing a shallow dive. Like it or not, he needed cooling off. The look in her eyes had heated him to the point of boiling.

When he surfaced, she was still standing on shore, looking exactly the way he thought she'd look—ready to bolt. Which was exactly what he wanted her to do. Nip this nonsense in the bud, that's what he planned on. A little more goading ought to do the trick.

"How come you've still got your clothes on?"

"I...um...isn't it cold?"

"Nah." He wiped his wet hair out of his eyes. "Just right."

She glanced toward Cletus and he thought, *Go for it. You know you want to.*

"Tell you what," he said, standing chest-deep in the water. "I'll count to three, then you make your choice. Either ditch the duds and join me, honey, or hightail it on back to the house and we'll forget this ever happened. Cletus knows his way back to the barn."

"One," he said and watched her bite her lower lip between her teeth.

"Two." *Go ahead, darlin'. Get out of here.*

"Three."

She closed her eyes and took a deep breath and he thought, *Bye-bye.* Until she reached for the hem of her top.

"Oh, hell," he muttered when the shirt came off. And then all he could think was, *Oh, hel-lo.*

Skinny-dipping. It always sounded so...playful. But what it was was intimate, Christine thought as she sat on the bank in her bra and jeans and tugged off her boots. It meant getting naked. In this case, it meant getting naked with a man.

Not just a man. A beautiful, well-conditioned, amazing specimen of a man who didn't think twice about stripping to the skin and flaunting himself in front of her.

Well, she wasn't a flaunter. Heck, sometimes she still undressed in the dark. And it may be well after midnight, but with the cloudless sky and the full moon and complement of stars shining down, it was far from dark out here. As a matter of fact, she felt as though she had a spotlight shining directly on her body.

Don't think about it, she told herself. *Just do it. It's what you want. It's what you need to do if you're ever going to break the pattern.*

Mouth pinched in determination, she finished pulling off her boots and socks, then stood and, with her back to the pond, unzipped and stepped out of her jeans. At the last minute, she reached into a pocket of her jeans and took out one of the packets of protection that Alison—dear, sweet, conscientious Alison—had pressed into her hand earlier today with a smile and a "Just in case."

With a deep breath Christine turned to face Jake and slowly walked toward the water.

"Nope," he said in that gruff, velvet drawl. "All of it or it doesn't count."

So much for hoping he'd overlook the underwear.

"Turn around," she said.

"Not on your life." His voice was sexy and low.

Another deep breath and she reached behind to unhook her bra. She couldn't look at him, but she knew he was watching. It was so quiet, she could hear the soft ebb and flow of his arms as he glided them slowly back and forth through the water. So quiet, she could hear her heartbeat and the soft snuffle of the horses where they grazed on the grass nearby.

She let her bra drop to the ground by her jeans, but she held her forearm over her breasts. She couldn't help it. One-handed, she tugged down her panties, stepped out of them, then tried to look casual as she covered the important parts below her waist with her other hand.

If he laughed, if he so much as snickered, she was going to drown herself.

He didn't laugh. He didn't snicker. He didn't make a sound.

In fact, even the sound of his arms skimming the water had stopped.

She took another deep breath and looked up. Met his eyes. And almost lost her breath.

He was just standing there. Not even smiling. His eyes were hooded with shadows, but even so, she knew his gaze was locked on her. Only when he swallowed and she saw the muscles work in his throat did she realize that he was as riveted by the moment as she was. She felt a power surge sweep through her again.

Feel the power, girl. Use it.

Buoyed by the memory of Alison's words, she stood straighter. And slowly lowered her hands.

This time it was *his* breath that caught. This time it was Jake doing the appreciating, as she'd appreciated the fluid muscle, the lean lines, the impressive part of his anatomy that distinguished him as a man.

She knew that he liked what he saw. When he took a step toward her as though it was involuntary, she knew that he loved what he saw. For the first time in her life she felt like celebrating the fact that she was a woman— a woman who intuitively sensed that this moment with this man was going to change her life.

Nine

"**H**oly mother of God," Jake whispered, so low that even he barely heard it.

She was so freaking beautiful. A moon witch. A night nymph. Pale skin frosted to shimmering silver in the moonlight. Pert, perfect breasts. An hourglass waist. Hips that were slim yet round and a soft little triangle of pale blond curls at the apex of her femininity.

Time out. Time out. Time out. The words kept racing through his mind as she walked toward him.

This wasn't supposed to happen. She was supposed to run. In the opposite direction. She wasn't supposed to be walking toward him, the water licking at her thighs, with that look in her eyes that was part uncertainty, part triumph and held all the trust in the world that he would know what happened next.

Well, hell. He didn't know. He hadn't planned on this part. He'd only mapped the evening out to the place where she lit out for parts unknown and this supposed walk on the wild side that he'd known in his heart she really wasn't up for was over.

Well, guess what? She was up for it.

Unfortunately so was he. He was a man. And like most men, he led with his libido.

"Stop," he finally managed in a gruff whisper. Not because he didn't want her to come any closer. Not because the water was just lapping at the underside of her breasts now and it was so intriguing to watch. He needed her to stop because he needed to make sure she understood what was on the line while he still had the wherewithal to muster up a shred of chivalry.

"Chrissie," he said, his chest feeling full, his hands aching to get a hold of her. "You don't have to do this."

She watched him for the longest time, searching his face before finally smiling. "Yes. Yes, I do."

So much for knighthood.

He was only so strong.

And he wanted.

He wanted her.

He wanted her bad.

He reached for her—hadn't realized just how much he'd been wanting to reach for her—and pulled her toward him.

Her back was warm and lean and wonderfully wet beneath his hands. Her breasts were buoyant and beautiful where they pressed against him, her nipples puckered tight, their velvety tips submerged in the little pool of water trapped between their bodies.

Her arms rose slowly to his shoulders as he backed them into deeper water. Her legs separated and wrapped around his waist, smooth as velvet, sleek as silk.

"Sweet, sweet heaven," he groaned and leaned his forehead to hers. "You sure you haven't done this before?"

She smiled, a little bit shy, a little bit pleased. "I'm sure."

He met her gaze then, loving the look of her by moonlight as that smile turned sly.

"I'm sure of something else, too."

"Oh, yeah?"

"Yeah. I'm sure that I've been missing out on a lot all these years."

Again he groaned.

"And I'm sure I want you to be the one to show me what I've been missing."

And damn if she didn't produce a condom.

Well, that did it. This hadn't started out to be a seduction. At least, he hadn't planned on seducing her. Just the opposite. He'd meant to scare her away.

Now he couldn't get close enough. Couldn't get suited up fast enough. Right versus wrong, reasonable versus rash. In the end it was no contest. And who was seducing whom got lost somewhere in the moment.

He lowered his mouth to hers, submerged himself in a kiss that was all wet heat and honest, uninhibited passion. He'd known it would be. The first time he'd kissed her, she'd given him exactly the same response. The second time she'd given him even more. She didn't have it in her to hold back, didn't have it in her to pretend. She was all reaction to his action, give to his take. And the more she offered, the more he wanted until he skimmed his hands down her back across her waist and filled his palms with the satiny softness of her sweet sexy bottom.

She made a throaty sound and squirmed against him. And he couldn't hold back anymore. He reached between them, made a quick pass of his fingers over her open, vulnerable flesh and guided himself home.

With his tongue buried in her mouth and her fingers knotted in his hair, he tilted his hips and drove himself deep. She gasped into his mouth, then settled herself with a throaty groan and started moving against him.

Bracing his feet wide on the bottom of the lake bed, he gripped her hips in his hands and helped her find a rhythm. Seemed he didn't have to worry about that because she knew exactly, instinctively what she wanted.

She wanted him hard. She wanted him fast. And she wanted him now.

"Easy. Easy," he whispered between deep, drugging kisses while his heart damn near beat out of his chest. "You're going to drown us."

"Don't care." Her lips raced over his face as she moved frantically against him. "Don't…care…"

Well, he did. At least, the part of him that wasn't going to be satisfied with having her and dying in the process cared a lot. With her mouth still mated with his and her hips still pumping against him, he stumbled toward the bank, half wild with the effort of holding back, half crazed with the way she was moving against him.

Finally, *finally,* he found dry ground. It was enough. He went down on his knees and, still buried deep inside her, let her do whatever she wanted with him. He was putty. He was clay. He was anything she wanted him to be as long as she didn't stop moving like that and kissing him like that and making those throaty little sounds that drove him beyond the limit.

"J-Jake." Breathless, she whispered his name. Restless, she rode him until he thought he'd go blind.

Just when he thought he couldn't take anymore, she shuddered and cried out and, with a long, sighing breath, melted into a puddle against his chest.

Gripping her hips in his hands, he went the same way she did, burying himself, riding with the contraction of her inner muscles, dying just a little from the sheer, pure pleasure.

He'd made a bed of sorts for them out of the towels he'd stuffed in his saddlebags—just in case. Christine lay naked as the day she was born, curled into his side, feeling boneless and brazen and about as wonderful as she supposed a woman could possibly feel.

Her head rested on Jake's shoulder, and his hand slid in a slow, steady glide up and down the length of her back.

It felt incredible to lie with him this way. Like Adam and Eve in the Garden of Eden. The smooth musculature of his shoulder pillowing her head, his heart rate slow and steady beneath the palm of her hand.

The night smelled of summer grass and a little of the leather saddlebags. And it smelled of him. Musky and clean and sexual.

"You okay?" he murmured, sounding just as drowsy and satisfied as she felt.

"More than okay." And though she was still drifting on the currents of her orgasm—my goodness, she'd actually had an orgasm—she couldn't wait to feel that amazing climb to the summit and the dizzying ride from the top all over again.

"Thank you," she whispered and, emboldened by the intimacy of their tangled limbs, pressed a kiss to his neck.

"Oh, no," he said, a smile in his voice. "Thank *you*."

She giggled. Giggled. Her.

"You don't understand," she said, pushing herself up on an elbow and looking into his eyes. His beautiful, beautiful eyes. "That's never happened to me before."

The lazy smile left his mouth. He stared at her. Long. Hard. "You were a virgin?" he asked, sounding so appalled that she laughed.

"Relax. I wasn't a virgin. I mean—" She hesitated, feeling self-conscious suddenly.

"What?" he said, touching a hand to her hair. "You mean you never came before?"

She nodded. Lifted a shoulder. "Pretty sad, huh?"

"Man," he said after a long moment, "those other guys must have been jerks."

"Guy," she said, again feeling self-conscious and horribly pedestrian and inexperienced. "There was only one. And...well, he said I wasn't very good at it."

"Major jerk," he said, hugging her again. "More like he wasn't any good at it, or I wouldn't be your first time."

It was a nice thing to say. And she realized he was probably right. She felt overwhelmed with this wonderful new feeling of power.

"Lots of firsts for me tonight," she said, rising above him. Twisting at the hip, she reached for her jeans, dug around for another condom, then grabbed his hat from the tree branch and put it on her head. "Never rode a horse before, either," she added and watched as his eyes went all stormy and dark when she placed a foot on either side of his hips and slowly sank to her knees. "Never rode a cowboy."

"Sweet thunder," he whispered on a groaning sigh as she dressed him then sank on top of him.

Okay, so he'd made a miscalculation, Jake thought the next morning as he drove to town. He'd thought Chrissie would run. He'd never dreamed... Well, he'd never dreamed they would do what they'd done.

He was an ass. A weak-willed, ruled-by-his-dick opportunist. He ought to be drawn and quartered.

So why was he grinning?

Well, hell. What man who'd experienced some of the best sex of his life less than—he checked his watch and rolled his eyes—four hours ago wouldn't be grinning?

Damn, did that woman turn him on. Those freckles were going to be the death of him. She had them on her shoulders, too. And on the very tops of her pretty breasts.

Still waters do, for a fact, run deep. Chrissie of the china-doll eyes and silky-smooth skin was a tiger disguised as a kitten. And soft. She'd felt so soft in his arms afterward, vulnerable and spent.

His mind flashed on an image of her wearing nothing but his hat and a smile, moving above him, and he damn near drove off the side of the road.

It was kind of a blur how they'd gotten back to the house. They'd ridden double on his mount. He did remember that—and all the friendly touching and kissing that had gone on between them, while Cletus had happily plodded behind them.

He flipped his turn signal when he hit a main intersection in town, then stopped at a light two blocks down. Waiting for the light to change, he drummed his fingers on the steering wheel and stared into space. She hadn't clung when it was time to leave, he'd give her that. When they'd reached the house, she'd kissed him goodbye and with a coy smile said, "If you think I need any more lessons, just let me know."

He wiped a hand over his jaw, contemplating all kinds of lessons he'd like to give her. Problem was, he wasn't sure who had been teaching whom last night.

A car honked behind him and he realized his light had changed. Gunning it, he drove toward the office, damning his slow reaction. Running on one, maybe two, hours of sleep, he could hardly see straight, let alone think straight.

He was mentally exhausted and clearly not in control of his faculties. It was more than enough excuse. When he finally reached his office, he shut his door behind him and reached for the phone.

He got her answering machine. "Lesson number three. Tonight. Seven o'clock. My place. Wear the black dress."

She wore the dress. And the silver heels. And, as he was soon to find out, that was about it.

"Hi," she said when he met her at his front door.

"Hi," he said and that was the extent of the talking for the next hour or so.

"I think you're teaching me to be a nymphomaniac," Christine said when she caught her breath.

She lay on her tummy in the middle of Jake's big bed, her dress in a tangled heap on the floor, her heels still on her feet. Beside her Jake lay on his side, his hand resting gently at the small of her back, his thumb stroking lazily along her spine.

"And so far it's going quite well," he said.

She smiled into the pillow, hugged it to her breasts and turned her head to look at him. He was smiling, too.

"You're amazing, Chrissie."

"Thanks. You're pretty amazing yourself. A girl couldn't ask for a better teacher."

His smile suddenly faded. He rolled to his back, crossed his hands beneath his head and stared at the ceiling.

"Chrissie—"

"No," she said, interrupting him softly. She had a pretty good idea what was going on here. Mr. Independent was starting to worry that she was pinning more on their "lessons" than he wanted her to. "It's okay," she said and reminded herself that it really was. "You don't have to worry. I'm not going to get the wrong idea about what's happening between us."

He turned his head and looked at her. Beautiful, beautiful face, she thought. So rugged and male and still unconvinced she meant what she said.

"Look. It's all fun and games. I know that. And it's fine. I don't expect more from you. I don't want more from you."

"How can that be?" he asked, his eyebrows pinched together. "Every woman I know wants commitment. Why not you?"

It was her turn to sober. She thought of all the pain commitment had brought her mother. Not that she figured Jake for a closet abuser—he was too gentle, too kind to ever be that. It was just that she never wanted to allow herself to count on anyone but herself. Life was less disappointing that way.

"I know the difference between fantasy and reality, Jake. Commitment doesn't necessarily mean happiness. And now that I'm better educated on life, thanks to you," she added with a smile, "I'm happy to go on and experience a little more. I don't need a serious relationship to do that."

He frowned again and she wasn't sure why. She'd thought reassuring him that she didn't have any long-term expectations would be a huge relief.

"Now," she said, feeling a need to lighten up things between them, "if you have any more lessons that you—devoted instructor that you are—feel compelled to put to the test, I'm burning to be enlightened."

Slowly, very slowly, his face lost that solemn look and he smiled. Sexy. This man was oh-so-sexy.

"Have I got a lesson for you."

He moved over her. The look in his eyes was so tender and searching when he lowered his head and kissed her. His lips were gentle, persuasive, as he settled them over hers, moved them over hers, softly caressing, expertly nipping, seducing her into very willing submission as he taught her more fine points of a kiss.

She could kiss him forever, she thought as he changed the angle and simply sank into her. Strong yet gentle. Tender yet forceful. He devoured her mouth, feeding her hunger, rekindling her need. She stretched beneath him on a blissful sigh when he left her mouth to give special attention to her jaw. The slight abrasion of his closely shaven beard whispered across her skin, making her shiver, making her yearn.

She arched to his mouth when he trailed a string of kisses—employing teeth and tongue and those amazing lips—along the length of her throat. She urged him toward her breast as he made his way slowly downward, his lips at her shoulder, his tongue flicking across her collarbone until she was begging, "Please, please." He finally took her nipple into his mouth.

Oh, did he know how to love her. He cupped his hand around her breast, plumping her for his pleasure, lifting her to his mouth so he could suckle and tease with the flick of his tongue, the whisper of his breath. She loved it. Loved how he knew what she needed.

When he moved lower, pushed himself to all fours above her and trailed a path down the center of her body with his tongue, she understood that she was about to experience another intimate lesson in loving.

The first touch of his mouth to her most vulnerable flesh was electric. She sucked in a harsh breath, let it out on a long, low moan and groped helplessly for a hold on the sheets on either side of her hips when he made the first lush pass with his tongue. And when he tunneled his hands beneath her bottom and lifted her hips to his open mouth, every pulse point in her body met there, between her thighs, where he made the most incredible love to her.

She closed her eyes, felt tears leak down her temples as sensations she couldn't begin to name assaulted her.

Pulsing, surging pleasure so intense, it radiated to her fingertips, to her toes, flooded inward again, propelling her to an orgasm so huge and so powerful, she bucked into his mouth, cried out in wonder and awe and disbelief. It seemed to go on forever and yet not long enough, and even as she started the slide down, his mouth caressed her, whispered praise, settled her.

When she finally came back to herself, he was moving up her body, his dark eyes intent on her face, his lips wet and swollen. She'd never seen anything so moving in her life. She reached for him. Whispered his name. Whispered her gratitude, then gasped on another storm of pleasure as he entered her, stroked her deeply and, on a mind-numbing explosion of sensation, took her to the limit yet again.

The next couple of weeks passed in a blur of fun and sensation for Christine. In between her busy schedule at the hospital and the time she committed at the Historical Society, she still managed to meet Jake often. They never seemed to get around to talking about Jess Golden's things, and frankly that was fine with her. She didn't want to end their...fling. My God. She was having a fling.

It made her smile just thinking about it. And about how often they made love. Jake was an inventive, sensitive and giving lover.

But there was one thing she always had to remember—he didn't love her.

As she drove across town on her lunch break one day, heading for Hellfire, International because Jake had called this morning and asked her to meet him at noon, she reminded herself of that fact. He did not love her.

It was something she found herself doing more and more often because, well, it would be easy to misconstrue the way he looked at her sometimes, the way he would reach out for no reason at all and touch a hand to her hair or to her arm, the way he made love to her. As if she was the one thing, the only thing, that mattered in the world.

Yeah, it would be easy to mistake all of those gestures for love. And that was a mistake she just wouldn't let herself make. Just the way she wouldn't let herself mistake her feelings for him as love.

"Hi," she said, poking her head inside his office after Janice had said she could go on in.

"Hi," he said, his face solemn as he took in her white hospital uniform. "Shut the door. Lock it."

"Is there something wrong?" she asked, feeling a little surge of alarm at the dark look on his face.

"Nothing's wrong. Unless you count the fact that I'm just itching to make love to you in that uniform."

She grinned when he walked up to her and put his arms around her. "You'd look a little silly in my uniform, but hey, if it trips your trigger, go for it, cowboy."

"Smart mouth," he said, then covered her mouth with his in a hard, demanding kiss.

The next thing she knew, he'd reached under her

skirt, stripped off her panties and deposited her on his desk. The shock of it, the heat of it, the urgency in him stole all reason. It thrilled her that he wanted her so badly. She couldn't get his pants undone fast enough. Couldn't get him suited up and inside of her soon enough.

It was all over in minutes. And it was incredible.

Panting, spent, she stroked his head where it lay on her breast, too satisfied to care that the desk was hard and unyielding beneath her back.

"Wow. That was quite a lesson," she ventured with a smile.

"Not a lesson. A pop quiz," he murmured and bussed her nipple with his nose.

She laughed. "So, how did I do, teach?"

"Well, I was going to make it a pass-fail, but since you obviously studied so hard, you get an A-plus."

Ten

"**Y**eah. I miss it," Jake confessed a week or so later as he sat with Chrissie in a booth at the Royal Diner one evening after burgers. They'd talked about a lot of things during the past couple of weeks, but this was the first time firefighting had come up.

Had someone else asked, he might have hedged the way he usually did. Brushed it off. Made some lame statement such as, "Are you kidding? Miss walking into a wall of fire as hot as hell? Do I look stupid?"

"Miss it a lot," he confessed because this was Chrissie. He caught her sympathetic look and firmed his lips because he just couldn't smile about it with her.

She was easy to talk to. Easy on the eye. Easy to make love to. He liked her. A lot.

But he didn't love her. And that, he told himself several times a day, was why things worked so well between them. All the silliness about "lessons" aside, things worked for them because they both knew the score. Love was not on the table. And it never would be.

"Tell me about it. What is it you miss?" she urged gently as she cradled a cup of decaf coffee between her hands. The same hands that could stroke him to arousal, ease him into sleep, amaze him with their gentleness.

He stared into space for a bit. The diner was quiet this time of night. Besides the two of them, there were only a few other hangers-on sitting in booths on the far side of the room.

Finally he shrugged. "I don't know specifically. I've always been an adrenaline junkie. Love the rush. Live on the thrills. And I hate it that my men are out there putting their lives on the line and I'm twiddling my thumbs on the sideline."

"Running the machine—the *business* machine—isn't exactly twiddling your thumbs. You give them everything they need to ensure they can do the job. You keep them safe in many ways."

"And I'd still rather be there beside them. Watching their backs. You don't know how often I've found myself heading for a fire—"

"You almost died," she interrupted. "You cannot risk

another incident with smoke inhalation. The additional stress to your lungs could kill you."

He nodded. "I know. Doesn't make it any easier."

She covered his hands with one of hers. Stroked her thumb over his skin, then squeezed.

"Is Connor as…oh, what's the word I'm searching for?"

"Pigheaded?" he suggested, needing to lighten things up a bit.

She smiled. "That'll work. Is Connor as pigheaded as you?"

He shook his head. "Connor is driven."

"He seems very serious. At least, the few times I've seen him, he strikes me as that way."

"When you grow up in the shadow of someone who was always perceived as the golden boy and the popular twin, it has a tendency to make you try a little harder."

"Had to be hard," she said. "For you, too."

Very insightful, this woman. Just one more thing he appreciated about her. "Yeah. I was who I was. Am who I am. Life's been easy for me. People like me. It wasn't that way for Connor. The old man leaned on him a lot— and it made for tension between us.

"The odd thing is," he added after a while, "Connor always was the smart one, yet our father put him down. Hard man, my dad. Never in all the years we were growing up do I remember him showing either of us any affection. Favoritism, yes, sadly. But not affection. It never bothered me, but Connor—well, he needed more. He tended to bottle things up inside, you know? Let them fester."

"And you?"

"Hell, I acted out by pushing things to the limit."

Okay. He'd talked more about himself in this one session with her than he ever had in the years he'd been married to Rea.

"What about you?"

"Me?" she asked, pulling her hands back, looking surprised.

"Yeah. What makes you tick?"

"Oh, well," she stammered, and he could actually see her withdrawing emotionally as well as physically. "Just your basic, run-of-the-mill childhood. Nothing remarkable there."

Chrissie was not a good liar. It shouldn't have bothered him that she'd lied. Aside from the fact that he'd just spilled his guts to her, it ticked him off that she couldn't trust him with the truth.

That's what people who loved each other did. They trusted.

Whoa.

His heart ratcheted to about one-twenty. Where had *that* come from? He didn't love Chrissie. He *liked* her. Had great affection for her. Admired her. Lusted after her.

But he did not love her.

He'd been there, done that. Wasn't going to do it again. Ever. He knew himself too well. He knew that he couldn't survive another hole like the one Rea had blown in his heart when she'd left him. He didn't want to ever again put himself in the position where he was that vulnerable to a hit.

And because Chrissie sometimes made him question a stand that had held him in good stead for several years, he figured now was a good time to get his head on straight again.

"What do you say I take you home?" he said, standing and digging into his hip pocket for his wallet. "I've got an early day tomorrow. I'm sure you do, too."

"Sure," she said, looking surprised by his abruptness but also as if she wanted to get away from this conversation as much as he did. "It's been a long day."

She didn't have reason to feel guilty about closing up on Jake just now, Christine told herself as she stood beside Jake at the cash register and Sheila Foster rang up the ticket for their meal. Still, Christine felt guilty for shutting him down.

She'd come a long way in the trust department. However not far enough to trust him with the truth of her childhood, even though he'd been honest with her about his feelings.

Intellectually she knew that she had no reason to be ashamed. The shame was her father's and, in some part, her mother's for not standing up to him and for not getting herself and Christine out of that horrible situation.

But still, the shame was as sharp as a slap from the

back of her father's hand, as acute as the verbal abuse he'd heaped on her with dump trucks then ground in with steamrollers. *You're not cute enough. Not smart enough. Are too much of a mouse. Always in the way.*

Someday maybe she'd get past it. But right now, well, it wasn't going to happen.

The little bell above the diner's door tinkled, and she shifted her attention there to see who had entered. It was Gretchen Halifax and some smarmy guy Christine knew she should recognize but couldn't quite place.

He was in his late thirties, maybe early forties. His hair was a dull brown, the same as his eyes. Small eyes. Snake eyes, she thought for some reason. Maybe it was the suit. It was a shiny gray material and made her think of snakeskin, covering a well-fed, bulky body. She wondered if he thought he looked the part of a smooth, savvy guy. Certainly the way he looked at her—big smile, come-on eyes—said that he thought he was quite the ladies' man.

She thought he was quite the loser but he hadn't figured it out yet.

Then again, he was with Gretchen, so what did Christine know.

"Well, well," Gretchen said when she spotted Jake at the counter. "If it isn't the backstabber."

Christine frowned. *Backstabber? What is she talking about?*

"Now, Gretchen," Jake said, sounding as patronizing as he could possibly be, "nobody is stabbing you in the back."

"Oh? Then what do you call running against me for mayor?"

Christine blinked from Gretchen to Jake. *What?* "Running for mayor?" Christine echoed, dumbfounded. "You're running for mayor? Seriously?"

"You know I'm a serious kind of guy," Jake said, glancing at her before returning his attention to Gretchen. "Not afraid of a little competition, are you, Councilwoman?"

"I'm not afraid of you. But then, I don't see you as competition."

"If that's the case," Jake said, smiling his best candy-eating smile, "it shouldn't bother you that I entered the race. See you around, Gretchen." Then he added, "Devlin," nodding to the man at Gretchen's side. With his hand at Christine's back, he guided her outside.

Durmorr. Malcolm Durmorr. That's who the man was, Christine realized from the muddle of her confused thoughts as she walked down the street.

"When did this happen?" she asked when they reached her car, still a little dizzy with shock and surprise. And with something else. Disappointment. Jake had done something major in his life and he hadn't even mentioned it to her. Hadn't seen fit to tell her. Which meant he hadn't thought she mattered enough to tell her.

"Just this morning."

She felt her stomach sink a little lower. Okay. So he hadn't told her. He wasn't obligated to tell her everything he did. In fact, he wasn't obligated to tell her anything.

It was just that, well, she'd thought— She'd thought she mattered more to him. And it shouldn't come as either a surprise or a disappointment that she didn't.

"Why?" she asked, feeling the need to fill the uncomfortable silence.

"Why run for mayor? You're the one who said it. I need to do something adult. Something civic minded. So I'm doing it.

"I don't like that woman's platform," he added as he opened her car door for her. "She wants major tax increases—for the local oil business as well as other businesses. She wants to cash in on increased tax revenues, and I am totally against that. Her platform not only affects my business but those of many of my friends and the people who keep Royal prosperous. She'd have a negative effect on the town—we'd lose business right and left—if she gets elected.

"Besides," he added, "I don't like her or her methods. And I don't like the people she runs with. Malcolm Durmorr—unlike the rest of the Devlin family—is a lowlife, a deadbeat opportunist. The fact that Gretchen keeps company with him just reinforces my decision to run against her."

"Well," Christine said, fighting that sinking sensation of exclusion that she had no right to feel, "good luck. And good night. Thanks for dinner."

She got in her car and drove off. Without another word. It was a little hard to talk through tears. And damn it, she was crying.

It made no sense. It made no sense at all that he hadn't told her about his decision. He had to have been thinking about it for quite a while if he actually filed the papers today.

His silence might not make sense unless he was trying to make a point, she realized, wiping her eye. And the point was she was not a staple in his life.

Now the really bad news. She hadn't realized until this very moment how badly she wanted to be.

She was in love with him. Damn her naive, foolish hide. Against all her own warnings not to, despite what she'd known about him going into this, she'd made a fatal mistake.

She'd fallen in love with Jake Thorne.

He'd hurt her.

As Jake lay awake alone in bed that night, he knew that he'd hurt Chrissie by not telling her about his decision to run for mayor. And the worst part? He was pretty certain he'd done it on purpose.

He'd kept thinking he'd tell her that he was seriously considering running, but in the end he hadn't. He hadn't told her because he'd known that if she found out from someone other than him, it would put their relationship in proper perspective. There was no future for them. Something they both knew.

So how come he'd felt as if he'd kicked a kitten when she'd looked at him with surprise, then hurt, then a dawning understanding? She'd known exactly the message he was trying to send. He'd wanted to make sure that she remembered—hell, he'd wanted to make sure that *he* remembered—what their arrangement was about. No promises. No future. Only fun for now. For as long as it lasted.

His cell rang, blasting him out of the doldrums. He was still picturing Chrissie's face when he flicked on the bedside light, saw that it was nearly five in the morning and answered his phone.

It was his site manager, Ray. There was an oil fire near Odessa. A bad one. They needed a crew. And they needed them fast.

He split the calling list of available men with Ray, then assembled his half of the crew. They'd all be there, on-site, within an hour—two max.

When he hung up the phone, he ran through a mental checklist. He hadn't missed any beats.

Everything was under control. Except his heart. It was waging a helluva war in his chest.

Each hard pump said, "Go, go, go."

But he knew he wasn't needed on-site. Knew he had no business at any oil-well fire. He wouldn't be able to stand back and simply supervise. He knew he'd get one whiff of the oil smoke, feel the burn of the blaze against his face and dive into the thick of things.

He dragged a hand through his hair, steeled himself against the need. Braced himself for the fight.

But not hard enough.

"The hell with it," he swore and vaulted out of bed.

He needed… He needed…something. Something to remind him he was still alive. Something to prove he was vital.

He needed Chrissie.

And because he needed her so badly and because he didn't dare give in to that need, he dressed in battle gear and headed for the fire.

Christine had the TV on in her kitchen as she always did in the morning while she got ready for work. She was rinsing out her coffee cup in the sink and about to shut off the set to head out the door when the reporter's voice stopped her.

"It's a bad one, all right, Mike." The reporter was doing a live remote from the site of an oil-well fire south of Odessa. "Hellfire, International—the Royal, Texas-based firefighting company—arrived in force about six o'clock this morning."

"Hellfire," she whispered aloud. Jake's company.

"At least two of the firefighters are being treated for minor injuries by EMTs," the reporter continued to say, "and it's not looking as though they're going to be capping this bad boy for a while yet. Let's roll some tape we shot earlier of an interview with Hellfire's head man, Jake Thorne."

Christine couldn't believe it. There was Jake. At the site. He was covered in smoke smudge and sweat, suited up in full firefighting gear, rattling off techniques and solutions and probabilities, then hurriedly excusing himself as he donned gloves and helmet and headed toward the plume of fire that boiled out of the ground like a geyser on a straight line from hell.

For a moment she couldn't breathe. Refused to believe that Jake was actually there. Not just there, on the site, but actively involved in fighting the fire.

"The fool," she sputtered aloud. "The damn fool."

It wasn't just a question of *if* he suffered more smoke or fire inhalation it *maybe* could kill him. There were no ifs or maybes about it. He was risking everything. *Everything.*

"And for what?" she asked aloud as she grabbed her purse and headed out the door at a run. "An adrenaline rush?"

Heart racing, she did something she'd never done in her entire career at the hospital. She called in sick from her cell phone. Then she floored the convertible all the way to Odessa.

She'd recognized the area from the news report, so she knew exactly where to find the fire. Still, the hourlong trip felt like forever. When she finally arrived, she was met with more frustration because she couldn't get to Jake. The police and local fire departments, as well as the drilling operation's security, were out in force to keep the area secure and free of curiosity seekers.

After parking several blocks away, she quickly locked her car and, at a trot, headed toward the source of heat. The heat factor grew outrageous the closer she went to the fire. So did the security.

"I'm EMT support," she lied, flashing the name tag on her uniform.

She figured it was the Respiratory Therapist title under her name that did the trick.

"Go on in. We've got triage and treatment set up over there." The guard pointed in the general direction of a pair of ambulances where several medical personnel were treating firefighters in need of oxygen, rehydration and first aid.

All of them appeared to be fine and getting the treatment they needed. None of them was the man she was looking for.

Working hard to control the tremor in her voice, she approached one of the firefighters where he sat resting on the tailgate of a pickup. "Where's Jake?"

He poured cold water over his head, then wiped soot from his face with a red handkerchief. "Down there somewhere," he said, nodding toward the fire.

Her heart sank just before a roar went up from the gathered crowd.

"She's capped!" someone shouted just as Christine turned and saw that the fire was out.

"Thank God," she whispered under her breath, then felt her heart take another dive.

"Man down!" The shout came from the center of the activity.

She didn't think. She headed toward the site at a dead run.

Frantic, she searched the weary faces of every man

who turned to look at her as she ran past. Ahead, a knot of firefighters hovered over the prone figure.

She pushed her way through them, grabbing one man's shoulder and shoving him aside. "Let me through," she snapped, then almost broke down and wept when the firefighter she'd tried to move out of her way turned around and looked at her.

It was Jake.

"Chrissie," he said, confusion and surprise clouding his face. "What the hell are you doing here?"

"Looking for you!" she said, not knowing whether to kiss him or hit him or bawl all over him. "I thought you were hurt. I—I thought you were...dead."

"Oh, sweet cheeks. Sweetie. It's okay. I'm right as rain. Old Ben here didn't fare as well, though. He might have a broken ankle."

The EMTs arrived right behind Christine and immediately went to work on Ben.

"Chrissie?"

Shock. She supposed she was suffering from a little shock. First from the scare. Now from relief.

"Chrissie," he said more gently. He turned her to face him, cupping her elbows in his big hands. "I'm okay."

His gaze locked on hers, his brilliant blue eyes searching from his smoke-smudged face.

Latent fear made her breath ragged. Frustration made her voice tight. "Why did you do this? Why when you know the risk?"

He had the sense to look guilty before he lifted a

shoulder, defiant, defensive. "They needed me," he said, but without the conviction to ring true. He knew what it could have cost him. So did she.

"What if I said I needed you?" She hadn't intended to confess. Hadn't wanted him to know. But now that it was out, there was no turning back. "What if I said I love you? And I was scared to death that I'd lost you? What if I said that?"

He looked as though she'd punched him and knocked every last breath from his lungs. He blinked, looked away, then back into her eyes. Finally he shook his head. He opened his mouth, but nothing came out.

"Yeah," she said, feeling very weary suddenly. And so lost. Lost in love with a crazy, foolish man who hadn't had a clue how she felt or what the thought of losing him had done to her. A man who clearly felt uncomfortable with her revelations. "That's what I thought you'd say."

She pulled out of his hold and started walking away.

"Hey… Hey, Chrissie," he said, catching up with her. "Let me walk you back to your car."

She laughed. No humor. Just sad acceptance. "Don't bother. Just…don't bother," she said, knowing that he was as uncomfortable with her being here as she was with the fact that she loved him.

She loved a man who didn't care enough about himself to ever care about her.

She'd hoped. Deep down inside she'd foolishly hoped that she meant more to him than a good time and good sex. Okay, that made him sound shallow and cruel. He was neither.

He was, however, exactly what she had always known him to be—a man who had no intention of committing to a woman. Especially not her. He couldn't have made it more clear. First by leaving her out of the loop on joining the mayoral race. And now with his total disregard for his own life.

No man who loved a woman would unnecessarily put himself in danger the way he'd just done.

Christine went to work. She came home. She cried. That went on for two days. And then she'd had enough. She'd survived worse than Jake Thorne's nondeclaration of love. And she would survive this, too.

But what she would not do was talk to him. She couldn't. She was too raw yet. And too needy for the sound of his voice. No, she would not talk to him. Cold turkey was hard, but it was the only way to get over him.

So she didn't return his calls or answer the messages he left on her machine. She did not want to hear him say things such as "It's me, not you." Or "I never meant for you to get hurt." Or "I thought we both knew there was nothing serious going on."

Well, nothing serious was going on. At least, not from where he stood. And from where she stood? Well, she'd eventually find firmer ground. She'd get over it. She'd get over him.

She'd get over a damn fool of a man who didn't have

enough sense to know that he could not take chances with his life for the sake of an adrenaline rush. A damn stupid man who did not know that she was the best thing that had ever happened to him.

Eleven

Jake waited five days. Five long, frustrating days.

Then he drove to Chrissie's apartment.

Stupid.

Par for his course lately. He'd pulled a stupid stunt when he'd suited up to fight the oil fire at Odessa. Okay. Water under the bridge. He hadn't intended to compound a gross error in judgment by going to see Chrissie.

So much for what he hadn't intended to do.

Man. Why couldn't he just stick to the plan? Even before Odessa he'd decided to cut off his relationship with her. He'd been worried that maybe she might be getting too attached to him. And he'd been right.

He could still see her face when she'd found him. Relief, anger. Pain.

Pain that he'd caused. See, this was exactly what he'd wanted to avoid. The possibility that she'd cry. The probability that she'd cling.

He flipped his left-turn signal and headed down Western Avenue, then stopped at a red light.

"Well, none of that has happened, has it, ace?" he muttered aloud. She hadn't cried. She wasn't clinging. Hell, the woman wouldn't even return his calls.

So why wasn't he happy about that? It was a clean break. Exactly what he'd wanted.

He scowled straight ahead. Five days had gone by since she'd charged onto the oil-fire site like an avenging angel, asked him what he'd say if she told him she loved him, then made herself as scarce as peace in the Middle East.

Love. She didn't love him. In the heat of the moment she'd just…hell, he didn't know. She'd been overly emotional, that's all. Clearly she didn't even want to see him anymore.

So why wasn't he as pleased as spiked punch about that, either?

For Pete's sake, he should be relieved.

The light changed and he punched it.

He should be feeling mighty fine that he didn't have to lie, make excuses or watch her cry. Or wonder if maybe she wasn't crying. Wonder if maybe she'd already moved on—asked someone else to give her "lessons."

There'd be no shortage of guys lining up to take his place, that's for sure. Since she'd quit hiding her beautiful assets, he'd seen the way other men looked at her.

His jaw started aching at about the same time he realized he was clenching it so hard, he could have crushed his molars into powder.

So, he didn't like the thought of some other guy looking out for her. Watching over her. Teaching her. That didn't mean anything except that he didn't want to see her get hurt.

That's what tonight was about. He pulled to a stop in front of her apartment. He told himself he was going to make sure she was all right. Just check on her. Make sure she knew what she was getting into with some of these other creeps.

But then she answered her door. Opened it a crack and frowned at him.

And he knew why he wasn't happy about anything.

He'd missed her.

He'd missed that sassy blond hair. Those crazy hazel eyes. Those whimsical freckles that drove him crazy with lust. He'd missed her spirit and he'd missed her spunk and he'd missed the way she looked at him.

But most of all he'd missed the best opportunity to tell her that he needed her in his life.

Since he'd figured that out just this moment—he'd never claimed to be the sharpest tack in the drawer—he cut himself a little slack.

And then he set out to make things right.

"We have to talk," he said.

"I, um, I don't mean to be rude, Jake," she said, clinging to the door, keeping it open only a crack so he couldn't walk inside, "but now really isn't a good time."

He froze as the light slowly dawned. She had a man in there.

"Yeah, well, I'm real sorry about that, but I'm afraid this can't wait."

He shouldered his way around her and stomped into her apartment. He stopped short just inside the door, ready to give whatever lowlife had moved in on his territory a real good reason to move on.

What the hell?

The place was a mess. There were newspapers spread on every inch of the floor. Plastic sheets were draped all over the furniture. And not a man in sight.

"You're painting," he said, feeling a huge smile spread across his face.

"I'm *about* to paint," she said, sounding a little testy.

That's my girl, he thought and started rolling up his sleeves. "I love to paint. What's this?"

She gave him a long-suffering sigh. "A paint roller."

"Oh, yeah. I knew that. So, where do you want me to start?"

"How about by heading back out the door?"

He smiled, picked up a paint can and started shaking it.

"This is ridiculous. I haven't got time for your games.

I need to get to the paint store before it closes and get some masking tape."

"You just run along and get what you need, sweet cheeks. I'll start without you."

She stared at him for the longest time. Then she swallowed and her eyes got a little misty. "I really don't think—"

"Go to the store," he said gently. "Before it closes."

After another long, searching look, she gave up and snagged her car keys. "If—if you ever cared anything about me," she said in a faltering tone that he'd never heard before, "please be gone when I get back."

Then she left, shutting the door softly behind her.

It was just like him, Christine thought when she pulled up in front of her apartment and saw that Jake's car was still parked in front. Just like him to do what he darn well pleased, regardless that she'd asked him to leave.

She cut the engine, let out a deep breath and told herself to just deal with it. Jake was Jake. He wasn't mean. He wasn't stupid. He knew she was hurting over him. And being who he was—Mr. Good Time, Everybody Likes Me—he simply couldn't handle thinking she hated him.

So his plan, evidently, was to make nice and put them back on friendly terms so he could live happily—and singly—ever after.

Fine, she thought, slamming her car door. He clearly wasn't going away tonight, so she'd have to play his game to get rid of him. She could survive it. As she so often reminded herself, she'd survived worse.

Head down, she trudged up the walk, then let herself inside.

And stopped cold when she walked into the room.

Eyes wide with disbelief, she turned a slow circle trying to take it all in. Good to his word, Jake had started the painting without her—only it wasn't the kind of painting she'd had in mind.

On the wall directly in front of her he'd painted in big sloppy letters *What would you say if I said I love you?*

She pressed her fingers to her mouth, walked farther into the room and felt her eyes fill with tears when she read the rest of his handiwork. Above the front window he'd painted a stick figure of a man with a huge, sad frown. He'd painted his name above it and the words: *I'm such a jerk.*

On the wall where the entertainment center usually sat was *Can you forgive me?*

Everywhere she looked, he'd painted a message. He'd painted a big, splashy heart with an arrow through it. Inside the heart were his initials and hers.

But the kicker, the one that finally had the tears overflowing, were the two words she never, ever figured she'd have from him: *Marry me.*

He walked through the kitchen doorway about that time, looking rugged and gorgeous and, God bless him, as uncertain as a skydiver on his virgin jump.

"Told you I could paint," he said, his gaze searching hers.

"You are such a fool," she said and launched herself into his arms.

He hugged her hard against him, lowering his head to hers. "A fool for you," he murmured, then picked her up, carried her to the wall that was foremost on both of their minds.

"Yes," she said, lifting her head long enough to kiss him. "Yes, yes, yes, I'll marry you."

"I think I could get to love this bed," Jake murmured into Chrissie's ear as they lay side by side, snuggled together like sardines in a can on her double bed, tiny in comparison to his king.

"You hate this bed," she said on a soft chuckle and wrapped her bare leg around his hip.

"But I love you and I love being close to you. This bed makes sure that happens."

She pulled back far enough to look into his eyes. "Say it again."

"I love you."

They'd made love. Then they'd talked. He'd told her about Rea, how she'd used him to get what she wanted, how she'd soured him on love and marriage. Christine had told him about her childhood and she'd fallen a little deeper in love when his eyes had misted with tears for her. He'd tenderly kissed the scar on her chin that her father had given her when she was six years old. That one tender kiss did more to ease the pain of abuse than years of trying to put it behind her.

And Jake had made promises. "I'll be good. I won't give you reason to worry about me. My firefighting days are over. Hell, they'd been over. The only reason I went to Odessa was because of you. You had me running scared, sweet cheeks. So scared, I did the one thing I figured would push you away for good. I figured you'd never forgive me for doing something so stupid."

Of course, she forgave him. They snuggled even deeper into the bed.

"You know," he said, reflecting on the events that had led them together, "if it weren't for Jess Golden's things, we never would have found the new you and me."

"That's right. We sort of forgot about that during the past few weeks, didn't we? You made me forget my name half the time," she confessed.

"I did that to you?" He sounded pleased and just a little too cocky.

She pinched him. "You know darn well what you did to me."

"Yeah. I do. Want to know something else? I never forgot about the lady outlaw's things. I think maybe subconsciously I was holding them as my ace in the hole."

"How so?"

He nuzzled her neck and kissed her there. "Well, why wouldn't I have turned them over if I really wanted out of this hot little thing we had going on? I mean, duh. Could it be any more obvious that I knew deep down that as long as I had them, I had some hold on you?"

"I don't care what the reason was. You will always have a hold on me," she confessed as he slipped lower and took her breast into his mouth. "Always."

Twelve

Logan Voss stared at Jake as though he'd said he'd grown a tail. "You're what?"

"Getting married," Jake said, grinning around a cigar similar to the ones he'd passed around to his buddies. Logan was late joining the poker game, so he was also late hearing the news Jake had shared first with Connor and then the other men at the table. "You gonna ante up or what?"

Jake and Connor, along with Logan Voss and Mark Hartman, were winding down from a meeting finalizing plans for the anniversary ball, which would take place at the Cattleman's Club on Saturday night.

Still looking stunned, Logan tossed his chip into the pot in the middle of the table. "It's almost too much to take. First you get respectable and run for mayor and now this. I've gotta think about this last piece of news for a while."

"Don't we all," Connor agreed. "I'll see your bet and up it twenty."

"I fold," Mark said and tossed his hand toward Connor, who had just dealt.

"Well, I think I can see that," Logan said. "Let's see what you got."

"Three ladies," Jake said, laying down his three queens.

"Guess luck's with you tonight, bud," Mark said as Jake raked in the pot.

"And don't I just know it. Thank you, boys," he said with a smile.

"Hey, Gavin," Jake said when the sheriff walked in. "You're just the man I wanted to see. Damnedest thing happened. Chrissie and I took that box of stuff I bought at the auction to the museum yesterday."

"What things?" Mark asked.

Jake explained about the saddlebags with the purse and six-guns and the map that Chrissie was so certain belonged to Jessamine Golden. "Looks like she was right, too," he added. "According to the historian at the museum, they're authentic. Those folks are as excited as kids on Christmas morning over what they called 'an exceptional and significant find' of Royal's history.

"Anyway," he continued, "you know that display set up to honor old Edgar Halifax?"

"The one your competitor, Gretchen, is so excited about?" Connor asked.

"Yeah. But it seems someone isn't as happy about the

display as Gretchen because they vandalized the hell out of it. Sprayed paint mostly. Wrote, 'It's all lies!' across the glass case."

"Already heard about that," Gavin put in. "I was just going off shift when we got the call. I sent one of the boys out to check it out."

"What's up with that?" Logan asked.

Gavin shrugged. "Total mystery at this point. Got another mystery on my hands that's taking priority at the moment. That's why I stopped in. I need your help with something."

"What's up?" Jake asked. "Or does this fall into the category of you'd tell us but then you'd have to kill us?"

"Actually," Gavin said, "I do have to ask for your pledge of confidentiality on this one."

Jake glanced at Connor, sensing something big was about to be revealed.

"We got the autopsy results back on Jonathan Devlin today."

"Autopsy?"

Gavin nodded. "Standard practice when there's even a hint of a question as to cause of death."

"Didn't know there was a question," Mark said.

"Yeah, well, like I said, there was enough of one. Long story short, the report got put on the back burner due to backlogs at the lab. Anyway, I just got it back today."

"Something tells me you're going to tell us he didn't die of natural causes," Connor speculated soberly.

Gavin cast a dark glance around the table. "Seems we've got a murder on our hands."

A stunned silence fell while the four of them absorbed Gavin's news and waited for him to continue.

"I had his house cordoned off this afternoon. For all the good it will probably do. It's going to be hard as hell to pick up anything from a crime scene that old."

"Crime scene? I thought the old man died in the hospital," Logan said.

Again Gavin nodded. "Look, I can't disclose any more information yet. Not until the state boys do their work. As it is, I'm sticking my neck out breaking this news to you, but I figure it's only a matter of time before the media gets a hold of it."

Gavin was right, Jake thought. Jonathan Devlin was a prominent figure in Royal business and society. Word that he was murdered would make fodder for the media for months.

"I just want you boys to keep your eyes and your ears open for me. If you see anything suspicious going on—"

"Like that business at the museum and the Halifax exhibit," Jake interjected.

"Or what's happening out at Nita Windcroft's," Mark put in soberly.

Gavin shrugged. "Hell, I wouldn't discount anything at this point. It's been almost a month since Jonathan died, so we've got a cold trail and a big, high-profile murder. I'm shorthanded and will be for a while with Wilson out on extended disability and Smith transferring to Dallas. To make matters worse, we've got a budget issue and a hiring freeze, so I'm dying here."

"You know you can count on us," Jake said. "And you

can bet that Tom Devlin will want to lend a hand, too, when he gets back to Royal."

"Okay then," Gavin said, looking and sounding weary. "I've gotta go. Let's plan on getting together on a regular basis and I'll fill you in on what I can when I can."

To a man, they watched the sheriff leave. And to a man, they knew they'd do everything in their power to help him.

Royal's one hundred and twenty-fifth anniversary ball was special for more than one reason. Besides the milestone event itself, for one of the few times in history, the private Texas Cattleman's Club was open to the public. That in itself was enough to bring out the residents of Royal to the gala ball in droves.

The posh club was renowned throughout Texas for its lavishly appointed bar, private rooms and extravagant ballroom. Those who attended that night and had never been inside the club were not disappointed in what they found.

Polished walnut paneling graced the foyer, rare Oriental rugs covered the floors. Gleaming brass fixtures and chandeliers dripping with cut-crystal teardrops adorned the ballroom. Presiding over it all was the one thing all club member held sacred—a plain wooden plaque over the door heralding the club's motto: Leadership, Justice and Peace.

It was a night for celebration. A night for sumptuous evening gowns and tailored black tuxedos. And it was a night that Jake hadn't even known he'd been looking forward to when he'd conned pretty Chrissie Travers into attending the ball with him.

She looked amazing. Her gown was red and strapless, and he couldn't get enough of looking at the contrast of all that vibrant crimson satin against her ivory skin.

"You are the sexiest campaign manager I've ever slept with," he said, grinning down at her as they waltzed around the room. He loved it that she'd thrown herself into the campaign, insisting that she handle his PR. Turned out she was a natural, too. He spotted any number of Thorne for Mayor—a Leader for Tomorrow pins on tuxedo lapels.

Personally he liked the pin she wore on the waist of her dress—Thorne for Husband.

"And you are the sexiest and the smartest and the best candidate for mayor I've ever agreed to marry. And unlike the other candidate, I haven't seen you cast a single glaring sneer the entire night."

He laughed and, as luck would have it, caught a glimpse of Gretchen Halifax as she danced by with Malcolm Durmorr. And sure enough, the look she knifed his way could have cut glass.

Gretchen didn't bother him. Jonathan Devlin's murder bothered him, as it bothered all of the guys Gavin had confided in—Mark, Connor and Logan. They had jumped on the bandwagon, too, and were actively campaigning for him for mayor—everyone but Gavin, since his own elected position of Sheriff kept him from campaigning openly. Still, Jake knew he had Gavin's support.

"Who's that with Logan Voss?" Chrissie asked when they waltzed by the bar area. "Oh, wait, isn't that the TV reporter who's covering the celebration?"

"Melissa Mason," Jake said, following Chrissie's gaze and seeing the reporter with Logan.

"They seem pretty familiar," she observed. "She's gorgeous, isn't she? I've seen her newscasts, envied her. She's even prettier in person."

"She's pretty enough," Jake said and waited for Chrissie to meet his eyes, "if you like that type. Me? I go for a hot blonde with wild hazel eyes and the sweetest body to ever skinny-dip in the lake on my south forty."

"I'd better be the only blonde who ever skinny-dips in that lake, Mister."

"The one and only," he promised, loving her more than he had ever imagined was possible to love a woman. "Always and forever my one and only."

He lowered his head to hers and kissed her, right in the middle of the dance floor, not caring that half the county was watching, and smiling as he did.

* * * * *

THE BODYGUARDS
They will not only guard your body,
They'll steal your heart and fulfill your deepest desires.
TO THE EDGE—May 2005
TO THE LIMIT—September 2005
TO THE BRINK—January 2006
From Cindy Gerard and St. Martin's Press

If you enjoyed what you just read,
then we've got an offer you can't resist!

Take 2 bestselling love stories FREE!

Plus get a FREE surprise gift!

Clip this page and mail it to Silhouette Reader Service™

IN U.S.A.	IN CANADA
3010 Walden Ave.	P.O. Box 609
P.O. Box 1867	Fort Erie, Ontario
Buffalo, N.Y. 14240-1867	L2A 5X3

YES! Please send me 2 free Silhouette Desire® novels and my free surprise gift. After receiving them, if I don't wish to receive anymore, I can return the shipping statement marked cancel. If I don't cancel, I will receive 6 brand-new novels every month, before they're available in stores! In the U.S.A., bill me at the bargain price of $3.80 plus 25¢ shipping and handling per book and applicable sales tax, if any*. In Canada, bill me at the bargain price of $4.47 plus 25¢ shipping and handling per book and applicable taxes**. That's the complete price and a savings of at least 10% off the cover prices—what a great deal! I understand that accepting the 2 free books and gift places me under no obligation ever to buy any books. I can always return a shipment and cancel at any time. Even if I never buy another book from Silhouette, the 2 free books and gift are mine to keep forever.

225 SDN DZ9F
326 SDN DZ9G

Name	(PLEASE PRINT)	
Address	Apt.#	
City	State/Prov.	Zip/Postal Code

Not valid to current Silhouette Desire® subscribers.

Want to try two free books from another series?
Call 1-800-873-8635 or visit www.morefreebooks.com.

* Terms and prices subject to change without notice. Sales tax applicable in N.Y.
** Canadian residents will be charged applicable provincial taxes and GST.
   All orders subject to approval. Offer limited to one per household.
   ® are registered trademarks owned and used by the trademark owner and or its licensee.

DES04R   ©2004 Harlequin Enterprises Limited

THE SECRET DIARY

**A new drama unfolds for six
of the state's wealthiest bachelors.**

This newest installment continues with

LESS-THAN-INNOCENT INVITATION

by Shirley Rogers

(Silhouette Desire #1671)

Melissa Mason will do almost anything
to avoid talking to her former fiancé,
Logan Voss. Too bad his ranch is the
only place she can stay while in Royal.
What's worse, he seems determined
to renew their acquaintance…
in every way.

Available August 2005 at your favorite retail outlet.

COMING NEXT MONTH

#1669 MISTAKEN FOR A MISTRESS—Kristi Gold

Dynasties: The Ashtons

To solve his grandfather's murder, Ford Ashton concealed his true identity to seduce his grandfather's suspected mistress. But he soon discovered that Kerry Rourke was not all *she* appeared to be. Her offer to help him find the truth turned his mistrust to attraction. Yet even if they solved the case, could love survive with so much deception between them?

#1670 HOT TO THE TOUCH—Jennifer Greene

Fox Lockwood was suffering from a traumatic war experience no doctor could cure. Enter Phoebe Schneider—a masseuse specializing in soothing distraught infants. But Fox was fully grown, and though Phoebe desired to relieve his tension, dare she risk allowing their professional relationship to take a more personal turn?

#1671 LESS-THAN-INNOCENT INVITATION—Shirley Rogers

Texas Cattleman's Club: The Secret Diary

When Melissa Mason heard rancher Logan Voss proposed to her simply to secure his family inheritance, she ended their engagement and broke his heart. Ten years later, now an accomplished news reporter, Melissa had accepted an assignment that brought her back to Logan, forcing her to confront the real reason she left all they had behind.

#1672 ROCK ME ALL NIGHT—Katherine Garbera

King of Hearts

Dumped by her fiancé on New Year's Eve, late-night DJ Lauren Belchoir had plenty to vent to her listeners about romance. But when hip record producer Jack Montrose appeared, passion surged between them like high-voltage airwaves. Would putting their hearts on the air determine if their fairy-tale romance was real, or just after-hours gossip?

#1673 SEDUCTION BY THE BOOK—Linda Conrad

The Gypsy Inheritance

Widower Nicholas Scoville had isolated himself on his Caribbean island—until beautiful Annie Riley arrived and refused to be ignored. One long night, one vivid storm and some mindless passion later…could what they found in each other's arms overcome Nick's painful past?

#1674 HER ROYAL BED—Laura Wright

She had been a princess only a month before yearning for her old life. So when Jane Hefner Al-Nayhal traveled to Texas to see her brother and a detour landed her in the arms of cowboy Bobby Callahan, she began thinking of taking a permanent vacation. But Bobby had planned to destroy her family. Was Jane's love strong enough to prevent disaster?

SDCNM0705